MADNESS

MORWITCH SERIES
BOOK TWO

JENNIFER REDMILE

COPYRIGHT

DEDICATION

This book is dedicated to my very good friend and writing buddy Alison Clifford, without whose encouragement and constant prodding this book would never have been finished. Every writer should have such an awesome buddy!

CHAPTER ONE

Jayce

I *am sorry, Jayce Raythawn, to be the one to tell you. The Dark One... is the man you know as your father, Thomas Raythawn.*

The Tree of Life's words kept playing over and over inside Jayce's head. He didn't know whether to laugh hysterically or scream bloody murder.

His own father was responsible for trying to destroy the mortal world. Seriously? Oh, and let's not forget the other mind-blowing news. According to some 'prophecy', he and Ellie were supposed to stop the maniac.

Unbelievable! How much more crap would they be expected to deal with before this all over? He dropped to his knees and covered his face with his hands, sucking in huge gulps of air. He needed time to get his head around all this. He felt his friends hovering nearby, but no-one spoke. The Tree's announcement had stunned them all. What must they be thinking? Would they still trust him, knowing he shared the man's DNA?

"I'm so sorry..." The words came out harsh and broken.

Ellie dropped to the ground in front of him, pulling his hands away from his face. "Jayce, look at me... please?" He lifted his head, his mind slowly clearing at the fierce determination and love in her eyes.

"Don't you dare apologise for what Thomas has done. You're not responsible for any of this. Jayce, your father is a complete scumbag. No surprises there. Except that he's worse than we thought. Come on, babe; we're supposed to be celebrating here. We just *saved* the Tree of Life and the entire mortal world... we're heroes. So, can we please go home now? I've had about all the bad news I can take for one day."

Jayce nodded and tried to muster up a smile, unable to speak past the huge lump in his throat. Ellie was right, as usual. He needed to just suck it up and move on.

"Welcome back," she said, wrapping her arms around his neck. His smile grew as her warmth and energy seeped into him, helping to restore his equilibrium.

"I love you," she whispered. "We'll get through this together."

"I love you too, gorgeous girl." Jayce held her close, thanking the Stars for the day they brought her into his life.

Jasper's hand settled on his shoulder. "Come on, son... time to go home." Jayce nodded, comforted by the old dragon's show of support. In the short time they'd known each other, Jasper had become a close and trusted friend. In fact, Jayce had come to consider Jasper more of a father than Thomas had ever been.

Right. Time to start dealing with this new reality. He got to his feet, pulling the woman he loved more than life itself up beside him. She smiled and squeezed his hand as they joined the others. They each bid farewell to the Tree of Life as Yvette grasped his other hand.

Oh, and don't think I've forgotten you still owe me a whole week of breakfast in bed. Jayce chuckled as Ellie's message entered his mind, an instant before a familiar jolt told him they were teleporting home.

REALITY RUSHED in to meet them the minute they arrived at Jasper and Isabel's farmhouse. Acrid smoke filled the old kitchen, seeping into Jayce's lungs. Wracked by coughing, his eyes streamed as he tried to make sense of his surroundings. A raging inferno blazed in the lounge room, the flames licking at the doorframe leading to where they stood. Jayce released Yvette's hand and instinctively wrapped Ellie in his arms. They needed to get out of there... *fast!*

Before he could so much as blink, Ellie teleported them out of the burning house and into the bushes near their own cottage. Realising Ellie was struggling to breathe, he relaxed his arms as they slumped to the ground.

Reaching out to wipe away the tears pouring down her face, he froze at the horror dawning in her eyes. What now? Who was behind him? He turned, ready to protect her from whatever danger approached, and groaned at the sight before him.

All that remained of their lovingly restored home was a blackened, burned-out shell. Thomas... again. Rage gnawed at his insides. The man was insane... he had to be stopped.

Jasper, Isabel and Yvette appeared beside them, eyes streaming as they coughed wretchedly.

"Are you guys... okay?" Yvette's wheezed, her eyes widening as she took in the devastation. "This is unbelievable. The council is way out of control."

Jayce shook his head and growled, raising his eyes to Jasper and Isabel. "I am so sorry. After all you've done for us... I can't believe... my father..."

Pain and anger flashed in Jasper's reddened eyes. "That is the last time I ever wanna hear you apologise for anything that man does. He is *not* your father Jayce... he's merely the monster who raised you. No one could ever hold you responsible for Thomas' actions."

A little of the pain and guilt encasing Jayce's heart eased. These people had done nothing wrong, and Thomas—he wouldn't think of him as his father anymore —had destroyed their lives out of spite! Jasper was right.

At no time in Jayce's life had Thomas ever earned the respect or title of being his 'father'.

Ellie stiffened in his arms and gasped, her eyes flying to her mother. "What about the aunts? You don't think—?"

Yvette shook her head. "No honey. I'm sure he wouldn't go after them. You left home well before this all started. Thomas would know you haven't been back. But I'll check on them as soon as we are somewhere safe."

Jayce snorted in disgust. "Somewhere safe? Seriously? Don't you get it? There's no such place anymore."

The horror on Ellie's face made him want to kick himself. "Stars, Jayce is right. Thomas will always find us. There's nowhere to hide..."

Yeah, way to go hero. He really needed to work on the whole 'strong, silent type' thing. Why couldn't he keep his big mouth shut? The tension in the air around him bristled with unspoken words. His friends were worried about him—hell, *he* was worried about him! He needed somewhere quiet, where he could breathe, and convince his brain to start functioning rationally again.

Jasper wiped his eyes, cleared his throat, and stepped forward. "Okay, everyone needs to calm down. Under the circumstances, I think our only option is to go to Sydney and talk to Amos." He turned to Yvette. "Can you teleport us somewhere quiet but not too close?"

Jayce caught the unspoken exchange between the older members of the group. What secrets were they hiding now?

Ellie frowned. "Ummm... who's this Amos, and what's in Sydney?"

"We'll explain everything when we arrive. All you need to know is that Amos is a friend, and we'll be safer there than here." From the frown Jasper threw in his direction, Jayce got the old dragon's unspoken message loud and clear. Ellie needed to believe a safe place still existed, and he needed to stop being such a dick.

"So, I think we should move a bit closer to the ruins." Jayce winced at the words Yvette used to describe their 'home'. "It might help mask our magic trail." No-one argued as they followed her lead. Jayce kept his head down, trying to avoid looking at the remains of the cottage. The 'home' he and Ellie once hoped would provide a sanctuary from those who hunted the 'renegade' morwitch and her dragon familiar was gone.

Had he known back then that his f... Thomas... led the hunt, Jayce would have understood that nowhere would ever be a sanctuary again. At least, not while the homicidal maniac lived.

Ellie

ELLIE SIGHED as Yvette teleported them away from the devastation. The charred, blackened dirt slipped away from beneath their feet, to be replaced by the concrete surrounds of a deserted alley. The muted sounds of a busy metropolis filtered in from nearby.

"Where are we?" Ellie laughed when she realised she'd whispered. Who the hell did she think was going to hear them?

"Chinatown, in Sydney," Jasper replied. "Amos is the leader of the rebellion we told you about, before the Tree of Life situation arose. He owns a resort not far from here, right in the middle of Darling Harbour. He offers short-term accommodation for rogue dragons and their families, until they can find something more permanent."

"O-o-kay. So, we're going somewhere posh. But, ummm... dyathink we might draw a little too much attention in the state we're in?" Ellie chuckled as they all became aware of their bedraggled clothing and soot covered skin. Walking into a resort looking like they just stepped out of a war zone probably wasn't the smartest move.

"Oh dear, Ellie's right." Yvette pushed a few stands of singed hair off her forehead. "I'm thinking it might be best if we were all glamoured before we arrive. I'm sure all our descriptions are in circulation by now. Ellie, do you think you can handle changing yours and Jayce's?"

"Ummm, sure. But I only ever removed and restored the glamours you cast in Darwin. How do I make new ones?"

"Close your eyes and picture the details of what you want the person to look like. The trick is to create every detail of the glamour before you start. And don't forget clothes..." Yvette winked and Jayce blushed furiously.

"Ummm, yeah... *please* don't forget clothes." Jayce grinned and her heart lifted. She'd been so worried about him since the Tree of Life delivered Her devastating news. His emotions had been see-sawing between guilt, anger, pain and frustration. Humour was a nice change.

"Any preferences? Age, race, hair colour?" she asked him with a grin.

"Well, anything would be an improvement on how the world sees me at the moment."

Ellie laughed at the thought of what their current glamours looked like. The world saw her as an old grey-haired scrubber, and Jayce as what he described as a shaggy old 'bum with a bottle-a-day habit'.

Fortunately, her and Jayce only saw the people they projected to the world when looking in the mirror. To her, he remained the gorgeous eighteen-year-old golden eyed hunk she fell in love with the first time they met.

She closed her eyes and conjured up an image of a suave, well dressed, middle-aged businessman. The perfect disguise for blending in with the crowd in a large city. Then she looked at Jayce and cast the spell to conceal his true identity. So how did she know if it worked? The Jayce she knew and loved remained unchanged to her eyes.

She shrugged and again closed her eyes. They'd find out soon enough whether it had worked or not. A picture of a thirty-something-year-old efficient looking secretary from a magazine popped into her head, and she cast the spell on herself. Perfect. Hopefully. Only one way to be sure.

She opened her eyes and held out her hand, using her magic to fetch a mirror from her old bedroom back in Darwin. She pulled Jayce over beside her, and together they stared at the strangers reflected back at them. A distinguished looking man with salt and pepper hair and an expensive suit stood next to an up-tight, neatly coiffured secretary. Their glamours were perfect.

"Well done honey." Ellie turned, her jaw dropping at the strangers in front of her. Her mother's voice came from the elegant Asian woman chuckling at them. Standing beside her, Jasper and Isabel were a couple of trendy tourists in their forties, complete with sun hats and cameras.

Ellie handed them the mirror and smiled. "Wow... this is gonna take some getting used to. Let's try not to get separated. I'm not sure I could find any of you in a crowd."

After much oohing and aahing over their new looks, they moved out into the busy streets of Chinatown. Ellie breathed in the new sights, sounds and smells around them. The delicious aromas wafting from the various restaurants made her mouth water and her stomach rumble. It felt like days since the sandwiches and coffee at the campsite the previous night.

A groan slipped out. "Can we please stop and eat? I'm starving."

Just when she thought everyone was ignoring her, Isabel dropped back beside her. "Sorry honey, not until we reach The Majestic." The woman patted her arm, giving her a sympathetic smile as Ellie's stomach continued to growl in protest.

"Right... so I gather The Majestic is the name of the resort?"

"Yes, about a fifteen-minute walk from here. Unless Jasper can manage to grab a taxi big enough to..." Isabel smiled as her husband's shouts interrupted them. A seven-seater taxi waited at the kerb. "Guess that solves that problem." Isabel linked her arm through Ellie's as they hurried toward the waiting vehicle.

2
CHAPTER TWO

Jayce

*F*ive minutes later the taxi pulled up out the front of The Majestic Hotel. Jayce tried to appear interested as Ellie bubbled with excitement beside him. "Stars Jayce... can you believe this?"

He frowned and opened the door. "I don't think I'll ever find anything unbelievable again after today."

Ellie's face fell, the joy in her beautiful eyes replaced by worry. Damnit, he'd done it again. Ellie needed his support, not this miserable negativity.

He shook himself, stepped out of the taxi, and reached back to help her out. Pasting a smile on his face, he used their telepathic link to send an apology.

I'm sorry sweetheart, I didn't mean to snap. My head is pounding and my stomach's in knots. I just want this day to be over.

It's okay, I get it. Hopefully this won't take long, and then we can enjoy some alone time. She returned his smile and squeezed his hand as they entered the impressive resort behind Jasper, Isabel and Yvette.

Jasper waved them toward the plush lounges scattered around the massive reception area. "Grab a seat guys, this shouldn't take long," he said as he continued toward the front desk.

Jayce tried to snap himself out of his bad mood as he sunk down into the comfortable lounge beside Ellie. She was like a kid in a lolly shop, eyes wide as she took in their opulent surroundings. He seriously needed to get over himself.

Jasper's voice drifted over from where he stood talking to a petite blonde receptionist. "Good afternoon. Would you please inform Amos Hughes that Jasper White is here to see him?"

The receptionist picked up the phone, dialled a number, exchanged a few quiet words with the person on the other end and hung up. "Mr Hughes will be right down Mr White." She beamed when Jasper thanked her and moved on to the next customer.

Less than a minute later, the elevator pinged, and a distinguished looking gentleman stepped out and headed toward reception, his eyes scanning the waiting area. When they landed on Jasper standing at the desk smiling, he first looked confused, then impressed, and then his face broke into a huge smile.

"Jasper my old friend? What a surprise. Why didn't you send word you were coming? And where's Isabel?" The smile on Amos' face failed to hide the worry in his eyes.

"Sorry Amos... spur of the moment decision. Isabel is sitting with some friends we brought with us so we could show them the city," Jasper said, gesturing for the rest of the group to join them. "Is there somewhere private we can talk?"

"Of course. Let's all go up to my office shall we. I assume you're staying? How many rooms will we be needing?"

"Three would be excellent, preferably all close together."

"No problem. Gillian, please arrange three suites for our guests under my name, and ensure the keys are delivered to my office when you're done."

Isabel moved up beside Jasper, smiling as she linked arms with her husband. "Aren't you going to say hello Amos?" she asked with a wink.

"Isabel? Goodness, it's been so long I almost didn't recognise you." He smiled warmly and returned the wink.

Yvette sauntered up to the group and raised her eyebrows. "Excuse me Jasper, but we'll probably only need two suites. I'm sure I'll be able to bunk in with someone."

Amos sucked in a sharp breath. "Yvette?" he said, opening his arms for a hug. "I suppose I shouldn't be surprised. You are beautiful, as always." She walked into his embrace with a grin.

Jayce smiled as Ellie stiffened beside him, a shocked expression on her face. *What? You never thought of your mother having a boyfriend?*

Ewww... don't even talk about it. I do not need those images in my head thank you!

"Perhaps we should move to Amos' office, rather than standing around here in the foyer attracting attention." Yvette's smile had a brittle edge. Then her eyes fell on Jayce, and she frowned. "Actually Amos, my dau... ummm, friends here received some bad news earlier today. I think they might prefer going to their room while we catch up. Would that be okay with everyone?"

Relief flooded through Jayce's overwrought body "Thanks Yvette... that'd be brilliant."

Amos threw them a sympathetic smile and nodded. He walked back over to the reception desk and returned with a key. "Here you go, room 1201. I'm sure we'll find a chance to talk later." The older man grasped Jayce's wrist and handed him the key.

Jayce lower his eyes to escape the man's intense gaze. What would Amos think of him when he found out what had happened? Somehow, he doubted the man would be as understanding as his friends.

"Right," Amos said briskly, turning to the group. "We can all ride up together, and we'll drop your friends off at the twelfth floor. My office is on fifteen."

Ellie

ELLIE BREATHED a huge sigh of relief as the elevator doors closed behind them. Jayce's depression worried her. It reminded her of when they first discovered their bond as witch and familiar; and the repercussions they faced.

She squeezed his hand as they followed the lushly carpeted walkway to room 1201. She'd decided to push the previous events of the day to the back of her mind and enjoy the moment. She tried to quell her excitement as Jayce opened the door and stepped aside to let her enter.

Her jaw dropped as she took in the details of the room. The entire wall in front of them consisted of plate glass windows with sweeping views of Sydney harbour.

"Wow... this place is incredible! Bit of a step up from the cottage wouldn't you say?"

Jayce groaned and moved past her to the lounge. "Please don't remind me of what we've lost. I feel bad enough." He dropped down and buried his face in his hands.

Ellie tried to ignore the old familiar anger bubbling to the surface. Not at Jayce, but at a father capable of doing this to his own son. Nope, the anger refused to be ignored. She moved to stand in front of him, hands on hips and a scowl on her face. "Jayce Raythawn... look at me!"

He lifted his head in surprise, and she launched. "Thomas Raythawn is a monster. And *despite* having to grow up with his presence in your life, you became a strong, caring, wonderful man, as well as a fearsome yet kind dragon.

Don't you see? This is exactly how he wants you to

react. He got away with bullying and manipulating you as a child, and now you're letting him do the same thing to you as an adult. Stop being ashamed of who you are. Your huge heart and caring nature are the things I fell in love with. Nothing will ever change that."

Her anger evaporated at the lost look in his eyes. She slid down on the lounge beside him. "I'm sorry babe... but you need to get over this. Remember when I shut down after Jasper told us the Councils would never stop hunting us? What did you say to me? Embrace the anger and the pain and use it against them.

You are Jayce Raythawn, someone who risks his own life to protect others. You could never be like Thomas... which is why he hates you and wants you dead."

His honey gold eyes filled with unshed tears, and he gathered Ellie into his arms. "Damn woman. Whatever I did to be lucky enough to find you, I sure am glad I did it."

Ellie sighed against his chest. It had worked... her Jayce was back.

CHAPTER THREE

Thomas

*T*homas hurled his half-empty glass of whisky against the wall, watching the liquid slide down the smooth surface to pool among the sparkling shards of crystal.

"What the hell...?" The damn Tree of Life was restored! How dare that ungrateful whelp and his morwitch interfere.

Thomas knew early on that Jayce would never be the son he always wanted. Not that he had been surprised—in the end, blood would always tell.

The boy took after his insipid biological father; the man Thomas killed in a supposed 'hunting accident' all those years ago. He should have gone with his first instinct when Arthur's grieving widow discovered she was already pregnant with her dead husband's child.

But as it turned out, the unfortunate situation she

found herself in worked in his favour. Thomas gallantly offered to be a father to the child, and raise him or her as his own, and Iridia agreed to marry him.

He leaned back in his chair, his mood lifting as he thought back to the day of the 'accident' resulting in his good fortune.

Thomas had waited all day for the perfect opportunity to kill the man. He craved what Arthur Raythawn had- a beautiful young wife, a seat on the Dragon Council, and a magnificent castle situated on extensive lands. While he, Thomas Reifer, possessed nothing but his looks, his ingenuity, and his thirst for power.

He saw his chance and moved quickly, raising his bow and pulling an arrow from the quiver on his back. The buck stood a little to the right and behind Arthur, so if his aim was slightly off it would be put down to an accident. He froze, the sound of the hunter beside him drawing his own bow giving him a better idea. As the other man released his arrow, Thomas cast a spell to alter its trajectory.

Arthur never saw it coming. He slumped to the ground dead, the arrow piercing his chest and stopping his heart instantly. Thomas had comforted the distraught hunter, swearing he would bear witness to the tragic accident.

Exhilarated by his brilliance, he relayed the news to the grieving widow, not as her husband's killer, but as his devastated friend. Iridia married him a month later, and he graciously offered to take the Raythawn name so her child would carry his father's name.

The memory faded and he growled in renewed frustration. He should have known better than to allow the pregnancy to continue. His *son,* and this interfering witch, would pay for their audacity.

He recalled his excitement when he first heard about Ellie bonding Jayce as her familiar. Thinking the witch a conniving schemer, Thomas looked forward to meeting a kindred soul. So he'd convinced the Council to put the bounty on her head as a way of bringing her to him, rather than having her killed.

Then the truth came out. The pair had willingly bonded and run off together. Rage had spread like a cancer inside him. He beat Iridia to within an inch of her life, convinced the woman would know of her son's plans.

Only when a truth spell failed to elicit any knowledge of Jayce's whereabouts, had he decided to let the hag live a little longer. Her continuing existence might yet be a weapon he could use against Jayce.

Thomas knew all about the enhanced magic Ellie and Jayce shared through their bond. He simply needed to think of a way to keep them apart. Separated, they were nothing more than a normal witch and dragon.

Not long after joining the Council, he uncovered the closely guarded secret surrounding the fates of the previous witch and her dragon familiar. The Councils of both realms had colluded to keep the condemned couple apart long enough to 'dispose' of them.

Thomas grinned at the irony of the Council's mistake. They unwittingly revealed their secret to the one person who cared. *Their son.* Thomas worked hard to hide his hatred and thirst for revenge, while secretly planning to avenge his parents' death.

Thomas was the *lovechild* born of the union between the ill-fated couple. Raised by his grandmother, he'd been hidden away from those who would kill him if they discovered he existed.

He grimaced at the term lovechild. He may have been conceived with 'love', but the useless affection never played any other part in his miserable life.

Thomas chuckled. In his mind, the only use for love came from the power it gave him. Especially over those stupid enough to let it rule their lives. Like Jayce's love for his mother—Thomas used that weakness to his own advantage for years. And now, if his suspicions were correct, Jayce was head over heels in love with this morwitch of his. Which gave Thomas exactly what he needed to destroy them both.

Whether or not their bond made them as powerful as his own parents, they had sealed their fate when they proved capable of undoing his dark magic spells. But the results of *their* magic required them to wield it together, while Thomas carried the powers of both races inside him.

He poured himself another whisky as a plan began to hatch. Such a simple solution, and it had been right in front of him the whole time. As his plan grew and took shape, his excitement at the effectiveness of their punishment made him dizzy with anticipation.

What he planned to do would be so much more satisfying than killing them. The snivelling whelp and his whore would pay for their audacity every day for what was left of their pathetic lives.

4

CHAPTER FOUR

Jayce

*J*ayce smiled as Ellie snuggled against him in her sleep. He felt like the weight of the world had fallen off his shoulders. *Of course none of this was his fault.* He needed to take Ellie's advice and move on. Allowing Thomas' actions to muddle his thinking just gave the man more power to destroy him, like he'd been trying to do all Jayce's life. Instead of wallowing in shame and self-pity, he should be helping the rebels find a way to bring the monster down.

Ellie's sleepy voice against his chest snapped him out of his reverie. "Well, those thoughts sound much more positive than earlier today."

She sat up and stretched her long shapely legs out in front of her. "I suppose we should find out where the others are and head up to this meeting. How long did I sleep?"

"Only about an hour. Don't worry. I'm sure they'll call when they need us." He pulled her into his lap and ran his hands through her silky, sleep rumpled hair. "In the meantime—"

As if on cue, the phone on the table beside him rang. Jayce cursed and reached for the annoying instrument.

"Jayce here."

"Are you feeling better Jayce?"

"Yes, thanks Yvette, much better."

"Excellent. Could you both please join us in Amos' office? Fifteenth floor."

"Sure, we're on our way."

Ellie groaned as he hung up. "Let me guess. They want us there as soon as possible."

Jayce grinned and tilted her face up towards him. "They can wait a few more minutes." He bent his head and caressed her lips with his own. She was the most precious thing in his life— his entire world. He sighed, wishing the *rest* of the world would just go away and leave them alone.

Knowing his wish wasn't coming true any time soon, he lifted his head and kissed the tip of her nose. "Oh, by the way, I thought you wanted to eat? If not, I can send the room service back—"

Ellie's eyes went wide as she scrambled off the lounge. "You ordered food? I can eat fast. Where is it?"

"In the kitchen," Jayce said, laughing at her exuberance.

Thirty-seconds later, she was back in bed, a mini quiche in one hand and a slice of cake in the other. "Oh my Stars Jayce, this is awesome. Thank you, babe. No wonder I love you. Aren't you gonna have some?"

"I ate when it first arrived half an hour ago." He stood and stretched his back. "Okay, we need to go. Stuff down what you can, and grab some for the road." He laughed as she ran back to the kitchen. "Although there's sure to be some up there as well. "

"I am *not* letting good food go to waste. Who knows how long it'll be 'til we eat again. Somehow eating always seems to be relegated to everyone's lowest priority when a plan starts to evolve."

Ellie

ELLIE SAT at the over-sized table in Amos' office and assessed the man at the head of the table. Amos exuded confidence and power, and Ellie understood why the man had been chosen as a leader. But something about him made her uneasy. About to dismiss her feelings as being negatively influenced by her mother's relationship with the man, she smiled when Jayce squeezed her hand. Great, now he's going to give me a hard time about my mother again.

Hey, I agree. Something's off about this guy. Jayce had read her thoughts.

So why are we the only ones who can see it?

No idea. But I don't think we should trust him, regardless of what the others think. Let's keep our opinions to ourselves for now though.

Amos had moved on to the next topic, and Ellie's ears pricked up. "So, now the Tree of Life is back to full health, we need to consider how to heal those who've been poisoned. The healing qualities in the soil and water will take care of most, except those who've lost interest in eating and drinking. I'm afraid there's nothing we can do for them."

Ellie stood so abruptly her chair flew backwards. "*Excuse me?* Did you just say you're sentencing all those sick people to death when we have the cure? Who the hell do you think you are? How dare you sit here in your ivory tower and play God! My aunts happen to be among those you dismissed as being 'irrelevant', and I refuse to let them die. If you won't do something about helping them, I will!"

Gratified by the shock on Amos' face at her outburst, she had to bite back the laughter that bubbled to the surface. Her friends and family didn't even flinch.

Jasper smiled at Ellie and gave Amos a filthy look. "Calm down honey. We're not going to leave anyone to die. I'm sure we can arrange for a community announcement on radio and TV. They can advise family and friends of those suffering from the wasting sickness to make sure they drink the water."

"Please excuse my lack of foresight Ellie. I'm afraid with all the information I received today I'm not at my best. Of course we will make sure the announcements are made." Amos kept his eyes down as he spoke, his white, tightly clenched knuckles negating the conciliatory attitude he presented. Ellie got the distinct impression the man did *not* appreciate her speaking to him like that. Well, he could just suck it up!

"Thank you." Ellie picked up her chair and sat back down beside Jayce.

Yvette placed a hand on Amos' arm and smiled at him. "I suppose I should have warned you. Ellie is very much like me. Outspoken, and passionate about protecting those she loves. Not only that, but we've also all had a huge day. How about we convene for now? We can meet back here tomorrow to discuss where we should go from here. This meeting has given us all quite a lot to digest."

Everyone around the table appeared to sag with relief, all agreeing with Yvette's suggestion. Jayce slid his arm around Ellie's waist and kissed the top of her head as she stood up.

Come on sweetheart, let's go. I think we might need to talk to Jasper and Isabel in the morning about this Amos and see what they can tell us about him. She gave him a grateful smile. Jayce's words were like a soothing balm to her frayed nerves.

Absolutely. I don't trust this guy as far as I could throw him, and my mother appears to be completely blind to any problems. Besides, I seem to remember some unfinished business from this morning?

Jayce pulled her closer against him, his golden dragon eyes smouldering. *You really are a wicked witch; you know that right?*

Jayce

JAYCE LAUGHED as Ellie jumped up and headed for the kitchen. He heard the *whirring* followed by the *ding* of the microwave. Carrying the plate of left-overs from earlier, she climbed back on the bed and huffed.

"Tomorrow morning, we are ordering the full breakfast. I can't remember the last time I ate a proper meal."

Ellie had fetched them some clothes, hers from her old home in Darwin and his from his old room in the Dragon Realm, and Jayce savoured the sensation of being clean again. As usual, the use of her magic had given her a voracious appetite.

"Good idea. How about we invite Jasper and Isabel for breakfast? It would give us a chance for a private chat," Jayce said, enjoying the reheated mini pie he managed to steal before Ellie devoured it.

"Yep, sounds like a plan."

"I might ring through to their room and ask them now, before they make other plans." He reached over and dialled the extension for their room.

"Hey Jasper. Would you and Isabel like to come for breakfast in our room tomorrow morning?... Great, let's say about eight then? ...Cool, we'll see you then."

Jayce hung up the phone and chuckled. "Jasper

sounded mighty suspicious. I got the feeling he knows we have an ulterior motive. It must be killing them having to wait to find out what's going on."

Ellie finished the last of the food and moved the empty plate to the bedside table. "Oh well, they'll know soon enough. Right now, there are way more important things on my mind than what Jasper and Isabel are doing." She giggled as she slipped under the blankets. "I am not wasting another minute of our alone time talking about other people. So... I was thinking we could...?"

Jayce rolled over and pinned her beneath his body. She squealed at his sudden movement and shivered at the smouldering passion in his eyes. He lowered his face until their lips were almost touching. "No more thinking necessary." He closed the gap between them before she could argue.

CHAPTER FIVE

Ellie

*E*llie woke in a lather of sweat. The nightmare had felt far too real, and her heart raced in panic. In her dream, they'd reached the aunts too late and found them already dead. Tears welled in her eyes at the thought of losing the two loving and caring old women who raised her. *Nope... not gonna happen on my watch!*

Jayce twitched in his sleep, as if his subconscious knew what she planned to do. He looked so peaceful, the strain of the last few days no longer evident on his face. Should she wake him and tell him about her dream? No, he'd never agree to let her go, and he had enough to worry about. Fine, she needed to do this on her own.

Slipping quietly out of bed, she headed for the bathroom, grabbing her discarded jeans and t-shirt from the floor. She wouldn't teleport directly there. Way too risky.

What if she landed at her old school? It wouldn't take her long to run to the house, make sure the aunts drank some water, and then head back to the school. She'd be back before anyone even noticed she was gone.

She threw on her clothes, focused on where she wanted to go, and the ground shifted beneath her feet. The school grounds were surprisingly well lit, and she held her breath as she scanned the area. Satisfied the place was deserted, she jogged toward her old home.

Memories of the night she first met Jayce made her smile. He had offered to walk her home. Nervous about walking alone after dark, she'd agreed. That seemed like an eternity ago.

Since then, stuff like that had become the least of her worries. She almost wished some dirtbag would jump out at her, so she could burn off some of the frustration crawling through her body. Would they regret ever meeting her!

She reached the front gate and crept around to the back door. A light shone from the kitchen, the back door wide open. Her heart hammering in her chest, she moved to the sink, filled a glass with water from the tap and tiptoed into the lounge room. The two old women sat unmoving, exactly as they had been when she scried them only days ago.

Crouched down in front of Serena first, she laid her hand against the old woman's face.

"Ellie?" the old woman said in confusion, and tears began to stream down her weathered old face.

"Sshh Aunt Serena... I'm here now. I want you to drink some of this water for me."

"But I'm not thirsty," Serena rasped through cracked and dried lips.

"I know, but I need you to do it for *me*. Just a few sips. Please?"

Serena nodded, and Ellie gently coaxed her aunt to keep drinking until half the water in the glass was gone. Satisfied, she patted Serena's hand and smiled. "Thank you darling. Now it's Emelda's turn.

Ellie repeated the process with Emelda, sighing with relief when she emptied the glass. They were both still weak and confused, but the water would eventually bring them back. Coming here had been the right decision.

"I'm sorry, but I need to go now. I'll leave you each a glass of water beside your chairs. Please promise me you'll both drink it all?"

"Of course, darling. But where are you going?" Serena asked, her eyes beginning to come back into focus.

"Mum needs my help with something. Don't worry, I'll be back before you know it."

"Okay sweetie. I love you."

"I love you too. Both of you, very much. Keep drinking the water and you'll soon feel much better." She smiled and headed back to the kitchen.

Ellie only made it to the doorway before a sharp jolt in her stomach knocked her to the floor. Intense pain wracked her entire body. Helpless against the nausea rising into her throat, she vomited onto the kitchen floor. *What the hell was that?*

Still heaving, she watched in horror as a pair of black boots stepped inside the back door. Lifting her head, she found a black-clad figure staring down at her. *Stars help me.* A bounty hunter.

"Well, well, well. I can't believe you were stupid enough to come back here. Seems my patience finally paid off." The raspy voice sounded like a hissing snake. A shiver ran down her spine.

Fighting against the nausea still plaguing her stomach, she sucked in a deep breath. *Think Ellie. You need to fight him.* Then she remembered her magic. Hah! Did the snake think she was just some helpless young girl? She growled and let her anger build, sending a power thrust at the hooded figure. Nothing happened. Her jaw dropped and terror flared anew. He must be shielded somehow?

She concentrated on slowing her breathing, knowing she needed to stay calm. There had to be something... Of course! She could teleport. Why hadn't she thought of it sooner? Focusing on the suite back in Sydney, she closed her eyes and waited for the ground to slip away. But like before... nothing. Sweat beaded on her forehead, rolling down her face as she tried to make sense of it all. Why didn't her magic work?

The man laughed, an evil sound that chilled her to the bone. "Don't waste your time darlin'. Your precious magic is bound. Didya really think I'd be dumb enough to let you use it against me?"

Bound? How was that even possible? Her whole body began to shake as the reality of her situation sunk in. She was trapped. And no-one was coming to save her.

She opened her mouth to scream, and the man lunged toward her. Before the sound could escape her lips, he clamped his rough hand over her mouth, his other arm wrapping around her waist. Without hesitation, she bit into his hand, kicking backward with all her might. He grunted, but didn't let go, his fingers digging cruelly into her flesh. His putrid breath was hot against her face as he pulled her harder against him, his gravelly voice growling in her ear.

"I don't think so darlin'. Thomas may want you alive, but he'll understand if I had to rough you up a bit 'cos you resisted. I'm sure you'd prefer I didn't ruin that pretty face of yours, but I will if I have to."

Ellie froze at his words. This man worked for *Thomas?* And he wanted her *alive?* She shut her eyes as the room began to spin. *Damnit!* This was her own stupid fault. Too stubborn to listen - as usual. And now it was too late. Knowing Jayce would never hear it, she sent him a message as she allowed the tears to fall.

Jayce. Please... I need you...

She groaned as the ground fell away beneath her feet. They were teleporting, and Thomas would be waiting at the other end.

Jayce

Jayce rolled over and reached for Ellie, surprised to find her side of the bed cold and empty. He frowned and opened his eyes, a surge of panic racing through his veins. When had that become his automatic reaction? He spotted the crack of light under the bathroom door and smiled, the panic subsiding. He seriously needed to get a handle on the irrational fear that swamped him every time she was out of reach.

He waited a few minutes in silence, but when no sound came from the bathroom, he began to worry. *Hey babe... you all right in there?*

Silence.

Elle... what's going on?

Still nothing.

He dived out of bed and opened the bathroom door. No Ellie. He turned back to the room and scanned the floor for her clothes. They were gone. He groaned and swallowed back the bile rising in his throat. Where the hell was she? He sucked in a breath as he thought back to the meeting last night. No. She wouldn't... would she?

He picked up the phone and dialled Amos' extension. "Amos. This is Jayce. I need to speak to Yvette please..."

"You do realise it's the middle of the night?" Amos grumbled.

"Yes, I'm aware what time it is." Jayce spoke through gritted teeth. He wanted to reach into the phone and wring the other man's neck. Calm... he needed to stay focused. "I'm sorry to disturb you Amos, but I'm afraid this can't wait."

"Fine. I'll put Yvette—"

"Jayce what's wrong?"

"Ellie's missing." Silence. "Yvette, I think she might be trying to help the aunts..."

"Of course. Why didn't I see this coming? I'm going there now."

"Okay, but come here as soon as you—" The line went dead.

A sense of dread wrapped itself around his heart. Images of Ellie hurt or...

He shook his head and dialled Jasper and Isabel's room. Jasper answered on the second ring.

"Jasper. Ellie's missing. Can you please come...?"

"We're on our way." He sighed with relief when the line went dead again. He needed not to be alone.

He hung up and sat numbly on the bed, angry with himself for not realising how upset Ellie would be about the aunts being left to die. But she hadn't mentioned it again, and he assumed Amos' apology had eased her mind. *Damn he was an idiot!*

He jumped up and moved to the lounge room, pacing the floor and running his hands through his hair. *Stars Elle... why didn't you at least wake me and let me go with you?*

He answered the quiet knock on the door a few minutes later and found himself enveloped in a huge hug as soon as he closed the door.

"Did you contact Yvette?" Isabel asked shakily.

Jayce nodded, comforted by the old woman's hug. "She teleported straight to the aunts' house. We think Ellie might have gone there to help her aunts. Damnit! I don't even know how long ago she left."

Jasper put his hand on Jayce's shoulder. "Don't panic son. I'm sure her and Yvette will pop back any minute, and we can all yell at her for putting us—"

Yvette appeared in the room with a haunted look in her eyes. "Serena said she was there earlier. She went into the kitchen to get them some more water and never came back out. This all happened at least an hour ago, so any magic trail was long gone. I'm so sorry Jayce...

Jayce's legs gave out and he flopped down on the lounge, dropping his head into his hands. "It's not hard to work out who's taken her. This is his way of punishing me. But *where* he's holding her is anyone's guess."

Yvette gasped. "You think Thomas *himself* is behind this? You don't think it might have been a random bounty hunter waiting at the house in case she showed up."

Jayce shook his head. "No. I'm sure it was Thomas. This is how he plays the game. He's more interested in the emotional torment he's putting me through by taking Ellie, than collecting some bounty."

"So, we'll just confront him and get her back," Yvette said desperately.

"How would you suggest we do that? We are hunted criminals. The minute we step foot in the dragon realm we'll be arrested. I know we're all glamoured, but Thomas isn't stupid. He has eyes and ears everywhere."

Yvette's eyes filled with tears, and then a smile broke through. "Wait, maybe Amos can help." She reached for the phone and Jayce covered her hand with his.

"Ummm... sorry Yvette, but I think we should talk about this between ourselves before we involve anyone else. Ellie and I both got a weird feeling about Amos. Something about him made us a little uncomfortable."

Jasper gave a huge sigh. "Is that why you invited Isabel and me to breakfast? I thought you had something on your mind."

Jayce nodded and frowned at Yvette. "Sorry, but we were worried your view might be a bit... ummm... biased. You know... because—"

Yvette blushed. "It's okay Jayce. I understand what you're trying to say. Jasper, have you ever had a reason to question Amos' loyalty to the rebellion?"

Jasper rubbed his chin and looked at Isabel, who nodded. "Well, there have been a few occasions we've been concerned about information being leaked to the Council. Amos has a great deal of power and influence, both here in the mortal world as well as the dragon realm. We've never been able to prove any wrong-doings, but I can't say I trust him one hundred percent."

Yvette sighed. "I must admit, his comment about not helping some of those affected by the poison surprised me. He knows Ellie is half-mortal, and her aunts are sick." Yvette's eyes widened and a look of horror grew on her face. "You don't think... no he wouldn't..."

"Think what Yvette?" Jayce spat through clenched teeth.

Yvette paled, her eyes avoiding his. "Do you think Amos might have been baiting her, knowing she couldn't resist going to help her aunts?"

"If he did, he'll live to regret it." He picked up the

phone and handed it to Yvette. "*Now* might be a good time to make that call Yvette."

CHAPTER SIX

Eleanor

*T*he girl opened her eyes, wincing at the excruciating pain in her head. Where the hell was she? Everything looked totally unfamiliar. Confused, she tried to remember how she got there. Agony knifed through her skull from her efforts.

Okay, maybe an easier memory. Like the last thing she remembered before... Wait... nothing? How could she have no memories whatsoever prior to waking up in this bed? No wonder the room seemed unfamiliar... she had no idea what *should* be familiar.

Panic surged through her. She couldn't even remember her name. How could her mind be completely blank? Wait, what if she didn't really wake up, and this was all part of some horrible nightmare? Although the dull ache in the pit of her stomach and the screaming pain in her head suggested she was either awake or in hell.

Her eyes flew open at the sound of a door squeaking. An older man with dark hair sprinkled with grey, and almost black eyes, entered the room and walked toward her bed. Nothing about him jogged her memory. But the concerned smile on his face told her the man must know her.

"Aahh, Eleanor dear, thank the Stars you're awake at last. I've been almost out of my mind with worry. How do you feel?"

Well at least she knew her name now. *Eleanor*. Damnit, the name didn't sound familiar either. She frowned and pulled the blankets up to her neck. "Ummm... I'm sorry, but who are you? I'm afraid I have no memory of anything before waking up in this bed. What happened to me?"

The man's face fell, his dark eyes watching her closely. "The doctors warned me this might happen. You had a bad fall down the stairs, and it seems your head injury resulted in amnesia. You don't remember anything at all?"

Tears filled her eyes as she shook her head, instantly regretting the movement as the pounding in her head intensified. So, she had an accident. Okay, well that explained the pain. "Excuse me, but... wh-who are you?"

The man sat down on the edge of her bed and tentatively picked up her hand. "No need to be frightened dear. I'm your father. Please don't stress over the memory loss. I'm sure this is only temporary, and everything will come back to you with time. Try to rest and focus on getting better."

So the man was her father, which meant she must be at home in her own bed. She held her breath, hoping the knowledge would bring back some flash of familiarity. But nothing came. Her mind remained as empty as a vacant lot.

The man—her father? —patted her hand and placed it back on the bed-covers. "The doctor also said not to try and push the memories to come back." Reaching into his jacket pocket, he pulled out a syringe and sighed. "This will help you to relax and sleep. We'll talk again when you wake up."

Lifting her arm, he pushed the needle into the vein in the crook of her elbow. Lethargy spread throughout her body as the drug took effect. It even seemed to ease the hollow ache in her stomach. Was that related to her loss of memory too? It hurt too much to think. Pushing the thoughts aside to deal with when she felt better, she sunk down into the soft mattress with a sigh.

Eleanor's last lucid thought before slipping into unconscious oblivion was a feeling she'd lost something far more important than just her memories. And what-ever it was, she *needed* to find it again. Maybe she would ask her father when she woke up.

Thomas

THOMAS' face broke into a satisfied smile as he pulled the door closed behind him. The troublesome morwitch no longer existed... replaced by a confused young girl who had no idea she possessed magic. The plan had worked perfectly. He wished he'd been there to see the look on Jayce's face when he discovered her missing... priceless!

Thomas licked his lips in anticipation of the 'rescue mission' his idiot of a son would launch. Jayce was so predictable it almost made him laugh. He often knew how the boy would react to something long before Jayce himself did. And this time, the young fool's actions would play right into Thomas' hands. Then he would destroy their bond once and for all.

Lost in the pleasant images of Jayce's downfall filtering through his mind, he failed to notice his wife's cowering presence until he entered the dining room. His good mood evaporated. He would not allow her to interfere with his plans for her precious son and his morwitch whore.

"Iridia, you were told to stay in your rooms until my current business transaction is completed. What are you doing wandering around the castle?"

"I'm sorry Thomas. I just w-wanted to ask if there'd been any n-news of J-Jayce?" Iridia's timid voice and downcast eyes disgusted him.

Thomas sneered, barely resisting the urge to slap her. How dare she ask him about her renegade rogue brat of a son. But then he thought of a better way to further punish the woman who gave birth to the ungrateful whelp. "Actually, I'm expecting a visit from him any day now. I'm sure he'll be very interested in my latest work."

Iridia's head lifted, her eyes flashing with fear. "But if he comes here, he'll be arrested and put to death. Please Thomas, you need to stop him!"

The words pushed Thomas past his limits of self-control. He backhanded her impudent face, sending her flying backwards until she landed in a crumpled heap on the floor. "How dare you ask me to do such a thing! The boy is a criminal, and as a member of the Dragon Council I will ensure he is dealt with accordingly."

Iridia huddled where she'd fallen, mumbling apologies through her tears. Thomas turned away in disgust, sickened by the pathetic sight. Reining in his anger, he concentrated on slowing his breathing. *Patience Thomas.* As soon the two interfering brats were taken care of, he could rid himself of her presence... permanently.

There would be an unfortunate accident, of course, and an image of Iridia's scrawny body lying broken and bleeding at the bottom of the stairs almost made him smile. Then, after the mandatory mourning period, he would find a mate who treated him with the respect he deserved.

"Let that be a lesson to you for disobeying my orders. Now return to your rooms immediately. You are forbidden to speak to anyone until further notice."

Thomas turned and left the room, heading towards his study. Damn he needed a drink! He shook his head, determined to push all thoughts of his simpering wife from his mind. Images of Jayce's agony as Thomas destroyed him and the love of his life resurfaced. He chuckled, hoping he didn't have to wait too long before the fool took the bait and came to the morwitch's rescue.

CHAPTER SEVEN

Jayce

*J*ayce fought to control his rage, pacing the room and waiting for Amos to arrive. He hated doing nothing while Ellie... He groaned and pushed the images of what could be happening to his beautiful girl away. He missed her random thoughts skittering around inside it, and his heart ached. *Damnit... he needed to find her!*

He'd grudgingly agreed to let Yvette and Jasper speak to Amos first, but at the knock on the door heralding the man's arrival he almost changed his mind. Isabel wrapped her hands around his arm and guided him toward the bedroom. With one last warning glare at Yvette and Jasper, he nodded and went with her.

Isabel closed the door and turned to him, her eyes sympathetic but firm. "Jayce, you need to trust Jasper and Yvette to find out whether Amos is involved. The man may be completely innocent, in which case we'll need his help to find her and bring her home. Blind accusations at this point will only make the situation worse."

Jayce stood in the small bedroom, his hands balled into fists in his pockets. The pain caused by Ellie's absence settled into a tight knot in his stomach. Of course, Isabel was right. Pity that didn't stop him from wanting to tear someone apart. Anger bubbled just below the surface, ready to explode any minute.

Isabel's eyes softened, and she placed a hand on his arm. "We'll find her honey. I can't even begin to imagine how hard it must be with your... Wait, can you still feel the bond? If Ellie were... well, the bond would be broken, wouldn't it?"

Jayce gasped. He should be able to feel their bond as witch and familiar. Surely something would be different? The hope vanished as quickly as it appeared. "Damnit, I have no idea how it works. No-one does."

"Maybe just try looking inside yourself. Listen to your heart and let it guide you."

Jayce ran his hands through his hair and finally nodded. He needed to at least give it a go. Closing his eyes, he concentrated on his heartbeat, searching for some sign of their bond. More like looking for a needle in a haystack! How the hell did he find something he knew nothing about?

He'd almost given up when he noticed something different about his heartbeat. Was that a faint echo? A second heartbeat? Ellie's? He sucked in a ragged breath.

"Isabel... I think I found it. My heartbeat seems to have developed an echo."

Isabel smiled and rubbed his arm. "Then she's fine. Wherever she is, we'll find her. To be honest, I pity whoever is holding her captive. I'm sure she's making their lives a living hell right about now."

Jayce felt like he could breathe for the first time since Ellie disappeared. She was still alive... and he would move heaven and earth to bring her home safe. Isabel had a point... Ellie was far from helpless. The thought of his fiery morwitch making Thomas' life a misery made him smile. She'd definitely give him a run for his money.

"Thanks Isabel. You're right, as usual. I'll try to exercise a bit more patience while we wait and see what Jasper and Yvette can find out."

As if on cue, Jasper's raised voice floated in from the other room. "You slimy dog. How could you do this? She's only a kid, damn you. She wanted to help us!"

Jayce reefed open the door, stepped into the lounge room, and took in the situation. Amos sat slumped in a chair, his eyes dazed. Jasper stood before him with clenched fists and fire in his eyes.

Yvette sat near Amos, shock and horror etched on her face, tears welling in her eyes. "I used a truth spell when he didn't appear as worried or surprised as I thought he should be. He admitted that Thomas threatened to declare him a rogue if he didn't hand her over. Thomas knew we'd eventually come to Amos for refuge. Which is why he had the houses torched. He's been one step ahead of us the whole time."

Jayce growled. "That's because Thomas knows exactly how my mind works. Taking Ellie is the best way to hurt me. Plus, he would know Ellie and I pose much less of a threat to his plans if we're separated."

He shoved his shaking hands into his pockets, fighting the urge to rip Amos limb from limb. The snivelling coward handed Ellie over to Thomas to save his own skin. So much for the rogues' pathetic plan for a rebellion. Their damn leader was working hand-in-hand with the enemy.

An idea began to grow. He glanced over at the dazed face of Amos and a grin spread across his face. "I think Thomas has finally made a mistake. Like I said earlier, strangers entering the dragon realm would be arrested on sight. But no one would think anything amiss if *Amos* happened to be visiting."

Jasper turned to Jayce with a frown. "Why the Stars would we trust Amos as a spy? He..." Understanding dawned in his eyes and he chuckled. "We send someone in who *looks* like Amos. Son, you're brilliant! While-ever Amos is safely tucked away here, there's no chance of him turning up and blowing the spy's cover."

Jayce nodded, turning to Yvette. "So, what do you think Yvette? Can you put a glamour on me that will fool them?"

Jasper shook his head and placed his hand on Jayce's shoulder. "I'm sorry Jayce, but it can't be you. It needs to be someone who's familiar with Amos' habits and life in general. Like me."

Jayce bit his tongue. *Of course,* Jasper was right, but he

couldn't sit around doing nothing any longer. "Fine. But you'll need to take me with you! I can use our telepathic link to find out where he's hiding her. Even Thomas wouldn't be conceited enough to keep her at our home."

Jasper seemed inclined to keep arguing, but then he sighed in resignation. "You're right. It would be best if you came with me. But *only* if we can find someone around here that Amos trusts so you can wear his glamour." Jasper turned back to Amos with a snarl. "Time for you to start spilling your guts, *traitor*."

Eleanor

ELEANOR. Nope, the name meant absolutely nothing to her. But at least the pain in her head had eased slightly while she'd slept. A tray of sandwiches and a glass of juice were laid out on a tray beside the bed. Damn, she was starving. She couldn't remember the last time she ate. Hysterical laughter threatened to bubble to the surface as she realised the irony of her own thoughts. Yeah right, as if she would remember eating and not her own name.

She pulled herself up into a sitting position, surprised at how weak she felt. *How long had she been here?* She waited for the light-headedness to pass and moved the tray to her lap. She reached for a sandwich and froze as an image flashed into her mind.

A young couple sat on a bed, the girl balancing a tray of food on her lap. The girl laughed as the man watched her eat, his smouldering, honey-coloured eyes brimming with love.

"Tomorrow morning, we are ordering the full breakfast," the girl said. "I can't remember the last time I ate a proper meal."

The image vanished. *What the hell was that? A memory?* Who were those people, and how had that memory penetrated the void in her mind? A sliver of unease slid down her spine. Why did she remember something like that, and not her own home and father? It didn't make sense. Unless the man who claimed to be her father lied? Dammit! Nothing in this whole nightmare made any sense.

The unanswered questions continued to pile on top of each other. But every time she tried to focus on anything specific, her head threatened to explode.

Someone knocked on her door, and she pushed the thoughts away for the time being. Her father, or whoever the hell he was, entered the room wearing the same comforting smile as the last time he visited her.

"Good morning, Eleanor. You're looking much better than the last time I visited. Are you feeling any better dear? Any memories?"

She shook her head and looked down at the tray, avoiding eye contact. She didn't want to risk him reading the lie on her face. Some inner instinct told her not to tell this man about the vision. She needed to continue to act like she still remembered nothing. At least until she worked out who to trust, and what was really going on.

"Never mind sweetie, it might take some time for your memories to come back. I thought you might like to sit outside in the fresh air for a while? Nothing worse than being cooped up inside all the time. Do you think you're up to walking, or should I call someone to help you?"

She shook her head again. "I-I think I should be able to walk. I'll just finish eating and clean myself up first. Could you give me half an hour?"

"Of course, dear. I'll be back shortly then."

"Thank you," she muttered as he turned and left.

Eleanor breathed a sigh of relief as soon as the door closed behind him. Then she threw back the blankets and inspected her nightgown clad body. Her body appeared to be about the same age and shape as the girl in her vision. Maybe the memory had been one of hers? Her heart rate sped up as she spied a mirror on the other side of the room. Only one way to find out.

The room started to spin as she tried to stand. She groaned and waited for it to pass, itching to check out the mirror. When the world returned to an even kilter, she swung her legs off the side of the bed and put her feet on the floor. She grabbed the bedside table to steady her shaking legs, gritting her teeth at her weakened body.

Damnit! What was wrong with her? Had she always been the weak sickly type? Was that why she fell down the stairs? She shook her head. No matter how hard she tried to accept what 'her father' said, somehow the whole thing didn't add up.

She stumbled to the dressing table and studied the reflection of the complete stranger staring back at her. Cloudy brown eyes set into a pale face, framed by long, wavy, black hair that fell to her waist. She sighed and slumped into the chair in front of the mirror, propping her face in her hands.

The girl in the image had green eyes and reddish-gold hair—nothing like Eleanor. The unknown sexy man from her vision sat in bed next to someone else. So why did that thought hurt so much? And why would she be there watching them in such a private moment?

Turning away from the mirror, she sighed in frustration. Okay, enough. Maybe the vision *was* just a scene from some movie. Time to stop creating ridiculous melodramas in her head and accept the truth. *Her* name was Eleanor, and this was her home. She had a fall, which resulted in amnesia. Whoever the people in the vision were, they had nothing to do with her life.

She seriously needed to get over herself and start working on recovering her *real* memories, instead of fantasising over a couple of strangers having breakfast in bed.

CHAPTER EIGHT

Jayce

*J*ayce paced the floor of their suite like a caged tiger. Ellie had been missing for two days, and they'd done nothing. He understood there'd been a lot to organise before they left for the Dragon Realm, but the waiting was driving him insane.

His eyes drifted to the three sleeping forms in the corner of his room. Yvette's spell would ensure they stayed asleep indefinitely. Gritting his teeth, and growling like that same caged tiger, he fought the urge to beat Amos and his cohorts to a pulp. But he vowed if anything happened to Ellie, he'd give those urges free rein.

"So Jayce, what do you think? Will we pass inspection?" Yvette called from the other side of the room.

Jayce's jaw dropped at the sight of Yvette and Jasper. He looked at the real Amos and his assistant Julia, and then back at Yvette and Jasper. They were identical copies!

Jayce grinned, his mood lifting. The waiting was nearly over. "Brilliant Yvette. Guess that means I'm next, huh?" He grimaced at the man sleeping beside Amos. "I can't believe, out of all the dragons in the world, I get to impersonate Riley King. The guy's always been a complete jerk."

He flinched when Jasper, wearing Amos' face, patted his shoulder. Sucking in a deep breath, he controlled yet another urge to punch the smiling face of his enemy. Jasper just shook his head and sighed. "Don't worry son. Hopefully none of us will be wearing someone else's face for long. Look on the bright side. At least Ellie won't see Riley's ugly mug when we find her."

Jayce shrugged and nodded to Yvette, who gave him a sympathetic smile as she cast the spell. He shuddered and looked around at the others. "Don't say a word. Being glamoured always makes me feel like I'm wearing someone else's skin. And knowing who owns this partic-ular skin is giving me the creeps, big time. Wait. What about our scents? Even with the glamours, if we don't smell right, they'll be onto us in no time."

Yvette bit her lip. "I tried to copy the scent as best I could. If anyone asks, we could say we've been ill with the sickness in the mortal world and our scents may be off for a while?"

"Yep, that should work. As long as our scents are altered, we should be fine."

Isabel crossed the room and enveloped Jasper in one of her bear hugs. Jayce couldn't hear their whispered words to each other, but they would be about safety and promises. His heart ached and his anger resurfaced at the reminder that he couldn't hold Ellie and comfort her with promises.

Next Isabel pulled Jayce into her arms and squeezed. "You be careful. And make sure you bring our girl back to us." Her eyes filled with tears. Jayce nodded, the words unable to make it past the lump in his throat.

Finally, Yvette and Isabel exchanged a quick hug, and Yvette held out a hand to the two men. "Amos... Riley... ready to go?"

Jayce grinned and pushed his anger back down as he clasped Yvette's hand. "Whenever you are Julia. Let's go find our girl."

Eleanor

ELEANOR SAT OUTSIDE in an enclosed courtyard and filled her lungs with the sweet fresh air. The delicious scent of honeysuckle and lavender wafted around her, and she sighed at the beauty of her surroundings. How could she have lived in a place like this and not retained some memory of it?

There it was again, the niggling sensation telling her something was off. Closing her eyes, she soaked up the early morning sunshine, determined to try and regain some of her memories.

But instead of memories of this beautiful garden, or her magnificent home, an image of an old cottage popped into her head.

The red-haired girl stood hand in hand with the gorgeous man from her previous vision. He bent down to pick her up and held her against his chest.

"Hey," she laughed, her eyes wide. "You're supposed to be married to do the whole 'carry me over the threshold' thing."

"Is that a proposal?" the man asked, his eyes searching hers for a response. "Because if it is, I accept."

The vision vanished, just like the last time. Eleanor's heart ached. The red-haired girl seemed so happy, the man gazing at her with total adoration. The images felt so real, as if she was there. Who were they? And why did her heart ache at their obvious happiness? Maybe she once loved the man too? That would explain the heartache.

She stood and shrugged off the unsettling images. Daydreaming wouldn't solve her problems - she needed to concentrate on the real world. A stroll around the inside of the castle might trigger some memories.

She turned to head back to the door and caught sight of a woman gardening in the far corner of the courtyard. If the woman lived here, she might know *Eleanor.* She laughed at herself for thinking in the third person. But her life as Eleanor was a total mystery, and speaking to someone who knew her might help. She squared her shoulders and approached the woman.

"Hello, should I know you?" Eleanor recoiled at the terror in the woman's eyes. "I... I'm sorry... I didn't mean to startle you."

The woman scanned the area and shook her head. "Oh please... you shouldn't be here. Please don't tell him you saw me. I'm not supposed to be here."

Eleanor frowned. "Tell *who* I saw you?"

The woman's face paled, her hands shaking as she dropped her eyes to the ground. "T-Thomas... He didn't want me to disturb you."

"Why would you be disturbing me? I'd love some company. Who are you?"

The woman swallowed and continued to look down. "I... I'm... Iridia. I ummm... work here."

Eleanor smiled and tried to ease the woman's discomfort. "Well, Iridia, I'm sorry if I made you uncomfortable. Did we not get along or something?"

"No, no... nothing like that. It's just... oh I don't know. Thomas insisted I stay out of your way. I'm sorry... I have to go now." The woman turned and fled through another door at the end of the courtyard.

Eleanor stood for a moment, undecided whether she should follow her. Iridia seemed terrified of her father, and she didn't want the poor woman in trouble because of her. Disappointed, she turned and walked back the way she came, sitting back down on the same garden seat.

For the first time, she wondered about herself before the accident. What if she'd been an over-bearing spoiled brat? If so, it might be better for everyone if she never regained her memory.

Lost in her thoughts, she jumped at the sound of her father's voice behind her. "How are you holding up Eleanor? Did the fresh air help?"

She gave him a fake smile and nodded. "Yes, thank you. My head is much better, and I'm not quite as weak." She fought to suppress a shudder at the man's satisfied smile.

Something about this man made her skin crawl, and until she found out why, she had no intention of trusting him. But who else could he be? She didn't believe he was her father, any more than that terrified woman she met 'worked' here at the castle.

So why would these people pretend to be someone they're not? And how the hell could she work out who was lying and who could be trusted, when she couldn't remember a damn thing? She rubbed her temples as the throbbing pain in her head returned.

Her father's eyebrows drew together in a frown. "I think that might be enough exercise for today. Remember the doctor said not to try and push the memories. Come, I'll escort you back to your room so you can rest."

Eleanor sighed and nodded as Thomas held out his hand and helped her to her feet. His hand felt cold and impersonal, not comforting as she expected a father's hand to be. So, if he wasn't her father, why the pretence? Wait. This place might not even be her real home. So why the hell was *she* even here?

So many questions. Her head hurt and her heart ached. The doctor may have advised her not to push to regain her memories, but *not* knowing the answers was seriously driving her insane.

Jayce

YVETTE TELEPORTED them to a large stand of trees just off the road leading to Amos' castle. Fortunately, the road, and the skies above them, appeared deserted as they strode toward the courtyard entrance. Jayce started sending messages to Ellie as soon as they landed. He didn't know what the range of their telepathy was, or if it even had one, but he'd keep trying regardless. If Ellie was asleep or unconscious, he wanted his voice to be the first thing she heard when she woke up.

Jasper strode across the courtyard and boldly opened the front door as if he owned the place. A servant appeared as soon as they stepped inside. "Master Hughes, I'm sorry, I didn't hear you arrive. We weren't expecting you today. You should have let us know you were coming and allowed us to be better prepared."

Jasper, wearing the face of Amos, gave the servant a condescending frown and waved his hand in dismissal. "Don't make a fuss, Henry. We're only here for a quick visit to attend to some business. I would prefer all knowledge of our presence in the realm be kept within the castle."

Henry bowed, a twinkle in his eye. "Of course, sir, as always I will ensure complete discretion is maintained."

"Excellent. There will be three for lunch," Jasper said, walking toward a door to the right of the main entrance. Jayce and Yvette followed him into what turned out to be Amos' office.

"Damn Jasper, awesome work man. You've got Amos' arrogance down pat," Jayce whispered, chuckling as he closed the door behind them.

"Don't get too carried away yet son. Fooling one servant doesn't guarantee success."

Yvette slipped her arm through Jasper's, and they walked to Amos' desk. "So what do we do now?"

"Hope and pray Ellie hears Jayce's voice so we can find out where she is and get the hell outta here."

Jayce kept up a one-sided conversation the entire time, the silence in his head making his stomach churn with nausea. Why didn't she answer him? What if they were wrong, and Thomas had her somewhere else? He flopped down on the lounge and ran his fingers through his hair, praying to the Stars to help him find her.

Elle... I love you... I need you. We've come to take you home. Where are you baby?

He'd been trying for almost an hour. What would he do if she didn't answer him? He didn't have a clue where to start looking for her. He shuddered at the thought of what might have happened in the two days since she disappeared. What had the monster done to his beautiful—

Wait. What was that? He sat bolt upright in his seat as a soft voice entered his head. *Ellie... is that you?*

Who the hell is this? And how is your voice inside my head? Her frustrated sigh echoed inside his head. Something was wrong. Why didn't she recognise his voice? *Oh great... so now I'm hallucinating. Just another side-effect from the head injury I suppose.*

CHAPTER NINE

Eleanor

*E*leanor woke from a deep sleep, relieved to find the pain in her head almost gone. *Of course it was.* Her overactive brain couldn't create more ridiculous melodramas while she slept. She sighed. Maybe she needed to listen to the stupid doctor's advice. Stop pushing, and let her memories come back in their own time.

Her thoughts came to a screaming halt when a strange voice entered her head. Seriously? Now she was hearing voices? She sat bolt upright in her bed, trying to make sense of what the voice was saying. He— yep, the voice had definitely been male—had rabbited on about coming to take her home. What the hell? She was already home. Holding her breath, she waited for the voice to go away. But it only got louder and more persistent. Her head started to ache again.

No matter how much she tried to shut it out, the voice

kept talking. Maybe she should answer him, or herself, or whoever the voice belonged to? At least that might stop her head aching. *So what* if she made a complete idiot of herself? Besides, she had nothing to lose. Apart from her sanity, which seemed to be questionable anyway.

Who the hell is this? And how is your voice inside my head? She held her breath - damn, she was doing that a lot lately. Nothing. Did she really think he would answer her? *I don't know why I'm even answering. Obviously, I'm hallucinating. Another side-effect from the head injury I suppose.*

Did the voice just gasp? Did imaginary voices do that?

Oh baby, thank the Stars I found you. What's this about a head injury? Are you okay?

Wait... what? Did he just call her his *baby*?

Hey, I don't know who you are, but I am sooo not your 'baby'. My father tells me I fell down the stairs and cracked my head, and I ended up with amnesia. Which might also explain why I'm hearing voices in my head.

She groaned at the possibility that this was the onset of insanity. Wait. What if she'd been insane all along, and her father was trying to protect her from the truth? Whatever... time to hang up.

You know what? This whole 'talking to myself' is totally crazy. Whoever you are, please just go away.

Eleanor waited in silence, hoping the voice would go away. But when he *didn't* reply after a minute or so, she realised she wanted it back. This entire conversation might be a figment of her imagination, but for some reason, having the voice inside her head soothed her, helping her to cope with the loneliness and confusion.

Ummm... hello... are you still there?

I am. The voice sounded husky, and maybe upset? Should she apologise for snapping at him? Fine.

I'm sorry. I didn't mean to be rude. My mind is pretty scrambled at the moment, but... well, your voice makes me feel better.

Eleanor groaned and put her face in her hands. Had she really just apologised to an imaginary voice in her head?

The voice chuckled. *Well, that makes two of us. Can you tell me where you are?*

Much more comfortable with the chuckling voice than the upset one, she smiled. *I'm not sure where exactly, but I'm in a castle, and I live here with my father. End of story. I don't remember anything about my life before I woke up a few days ago.*

The voice almost growled at her words. What was he upset about this time? Had she said something wrong? Well, whatever his problem was, he could just suck it up!

Sorry about the growling thing. What's your father's name?

Ummm... Thomas. And I'm Eleanor. The only other person I've met is a woman called Iridia, who said she worked here. Hey, why did you keep calling me Ellie before? Is that a nickname or something?

Can you give me a minute? I'll be right back.

Okay, now he sounded *majorly* upset. Almost as if he were gritting his teeth. The absurdity of the whole conversation made her giggle. If this really was all in her imagination, she was obviously a master at imitating voices. Oops, she almost forgot to answer him.

Sure, I'm not going anywhere.

She took a deep breath and tried to assess the situation rationally. Even if the voice was imaginary, talking to him might still be better than having no-one to talk to. He might even be able to help her solve some of her problems. She could ask him about the visions and share her doubts and fears about her father and her lack of memories. Yep, that's what she'd do. Oh, and a name would be good. Calling him 'the voice' made everything somehow weirder.

Hey, sorry about that. I'm back.

All good. Hey, do you have a name?

It's Jayce. Jayce Raythawn.

Why does that name sound familiar when my own name doesn't? Weird huh? So... I don't suppose you've got dark hair and honey-coloured eyes?

The voice... Jayce... gasped. *Yes, I do... why do you ask?*

I keep having these visions or something, and I think you're in them. You're with a woman with red hair and green eyes. Is she your girlfriend?

My fiancé... yes. You didn't recognise her? Did she not look a bit like you?

Eleanor giggled. *Yeah right. 'Cos my black hair and brown eyes look so much like her. Why would I recognise her? Do I know her... and you?*

The voice growled again. *Damnit Elle... What's he done to you? Why don't you just use your powers and teleport outta there?*

Okay, upset she could handle, but this angry voice

scared the hell out of her. The whole thing was getting way too weird.

Ummm... I don't have a clue what you're talking about, and I think it might be time for you to go. You're scaring me.

The voice went silent. He was gone. She slumped back on her pillow and curled up into a ball. The silence in her head made her feel empty and alone again. She missed the 'many tones of Jayce' already. Was this what insanity felt like? Tears welled up in her eyes and spilled down over her cheeks. Would she ever be normal again?

She was almost asleep when the husky, pain-filled voice re-entered her mind. *I'm so sorry sweetheart. I didn't mean to scare you. I promise I'll make everything better again soon. You can trust me... and know that I will never stop loving you.*

Jayce

JAYCE LEAPT off the lounge with a roar. "Damnit, I'm gonna kill him! She doesn't remember who she is, or ever having magic. She sounds so lost and scared... and I can't help her!"

Jayce had told Yvette and Jasper about their conversation when he blocked Ellie earlier. He'd taken a few minutes to quell the anger raging through him, and then ended up letting it out anyway. Ellie had actually been scared of him! Shame washed over him at his inability to hold back his frustration and anger. If he was going to save her, he needed to stay calm and focused

Yvette frowned and looked at him. "Okay, it sounds like Thomas cast a memory wiping spell on her. But we don't know whether her magic is bound. What I don't understand, is how she heard your message? Unless this is something to do with your bond. Damnit, I wish we knew more about how that worked. I don't know what to do."

Jayce threw his hands in the air. What was the point of discussing the how's and why's of what happened. None of that would help him rescue Ellie. So, no more standing around like a useless moron. "As far as I'm concerned there's only one thing *to* do. Ellie is being held captive in my home. So we go and bring her out. End of story!"

Jasper moved toward him and placed a calming hand on his shoulder. "First thing you need to do son is calm down. Going off half-cocked will only make things worse. Thomas is expecting you to come after her, and whether you're glamoured or not, you'll be arrested on sight. We need to think of another way to get her out." Jasper took a deep breath and looked into Jayce's eyes.

"The most important thing for you to do now is regain Ellie's trust. You're the only one who can convince her that Thomas is lying, and we are the good guys. But it will take a lot of patience and time. Can you handle that?"

Jayce ran his hands through his hair and nodded. "He's also put a glamour on her. She seriously thinks she has black hair and brown eyes. Oh, and she said she had a couple of visions or something and asked me about the red-haired girl I was with."

"Wait... what?" Yvette's eyes almost popped out of her head. "Th-that should be impossible. The spell is supposed to completely wipe all memories. I knew Ellie was powerful, but it must be her bond with you that's allowing them to break through. The same way your telepathic link still works. You need to try and trigger a few more. The more memories you share, the easier it will be for her to trust you."

A soft knock on the door heralded the arrival of the servant, Henry. "Excuse me sir, lunch is ready whenever you are. Would you prefer to eat in the dining room or the courtyard?"

"The courtyard will be fine, thank you Henry. We'll be there shortly."

Yvette waited for Henry to close the door behind him before she spoke, her eyes sparkling with excitement. "Jayce, the more I think about it, the more it makes sense. I think you might be able to reverse the glamour on Ellie. Even if her magic is bound, your bond may be strong enough to help her gain access to the magic you share.

If you can convince Ellie to trust you, I can give you the spell to restore her memory. Remember when you said the words of the healing spell, and she repeated them to heal herself? Your combined strength made the wound appear weeks old."

She chuckled and shook her head. "Like we keep saying, no one has any idea what you're capable of. What do you think? Worth a try?"

Thomas might have made yet another fatal error. Hope pushed all other thoughts from Jayce's mind. Thomas didn't know about their telepathic link, and even if he did, he would never consider their bond powerful enough to break through his spell. Now he just needed to convince Ellie to trust him, and believe she had the power to get herself out of there!

CHAPTER TEN

Eleanor

*O*pening her eyes to find nothing changed, Eleanor wanted to scream in frustration. Still no memories, and nothing looked even remotely familiar. She just wanted the nightmare to be over. But at least she had one *new* memory to think about. The voice—Jayce. Did he really say he loved her... or were the words just part of another dream? What if *her* love for him existed somewhere in her lost memories?

Sick of not knowing who to trust or believe, anger bubbled and rose to the surface like an old friend. Finally, something that felt familiar. So what *if she didn't remember anything before the accident?* Something very wrong was going on here, and she needed to sort out the lies from the reality. Time to stop sitting back and accepting whatever scraps of information fell at her feet.

Right. First, she needed to analyse the way she felt

about 'her father'. Why did the man make her skin crawl? Surely that wasn't a normal reaction of a daughter to her father? He must have done something bad in her past to make her feel this way. But what? No new memories or visions surfaced. She sighed and moved on.

Okay, what about Iridia? The woman appeared to be terrified of something or someone... and everything pointed to it being Thomas. Eleanor's skin didn't crawl when *Iridia* spoke to her, like it did with father, so why would Thomas insist Iridia stay away from her? She waited, nothing from those thoughts either. This didn't make any sense!

A new thought weaved its way into her mind. What if this place was an insane asylum, and Iridia was a fellow patient? She shuddered and pushed the thought away. Thankfully, no visions arose from *those* thoughts.

Finally, she allowed herself to think about the voice— Jayce. The thoughts had been clammering to be heard the whole time. But she'd kept pushing them away, refusing to listen until she analysed her reaction to the only two *real* people in her life.

Okay, time to open the door to the Jayce thoughts. She smiled as she linked her memories of his voice to the image of his smiling face, love pouring from his honey-gold eyes. But that love had been for someone else. A woman with red hair and green eyes. So why did he say he loved *her*, Eleanor, or Ellie as he called her?

Aaarrgh! More questions without answers. How come she could hear Jayce's voice in her head in the first place? Surely it must mean they had some kind of connection?

She groaned, surprised by how much she wanted to be the one in the visions. Apart from anything else, the guy was seriously hot!

Thank you... you're pretty damned hot yourself.

Eleanor's face burned. How long had he been listening to her thoughts? An image of him kissing the red-haired woman flashed into her mind. Her heart contracted with pain. Woah, did she just have an attack of jealousy? Why would she be jealous? She didn't even know the guy... did she?

Elle... I get that this is all confusing, but I need you to trust me. It's the only way we can fix what's going on. Would you like your memories back?

Eleanor gasped in shock as a sense of longing filled her entire body. She wanted to be with this man more than life itself. So what about the redhead? He was *engaged* to her for crying out loud. He didn't love Eleanor, he loved *her!*

I don't understand any of this. Why do I feel so drawn to you, when the images always show you with another woman?

The voice... Jayce... sighed. This was a way different tone to their last conversation. Husky and frustrated. The guy's emotions were a mess.

The only way I can explain any of this is if you trust me enough not to lie to you. Do you think you can do that babe?

His words caressed her mind. Damn, that sounded corny. But she couldn't describe the effect of his words any other way. The longing to touch him became almost unbearable.

I think so. Something isn't right about what's going on here, so maybe you can help me make sense of it all.

A new vision flashed into her head. Jayce cradled a woman in his arms. The woman's face looked like the redhead from her previous visions, but this time she had black hair and brown eyes. Wait. The woman in his arms was her! Eleanor. Whoa... how the hell did he change it? He didn't even know what she looked like. Or had *she* changed it because she wanted it to be her?

Did you see it Elle? Did you see me holding you? You are the redhead. Thomas messed with your mind so you can't see who you really are.

She jumped out of bed and ran to the mirror. She imagined her face with green eyes and red hair. *Well I'll be damned.* For the first time since she woke up after her accident, something made sense. No wonder she had so many memories with Jayce... *She* was the redhead all along. So how did her fath—Thomas—change how she looked?

Jayce chuckled. She kept forgetting he could hear her every thought. *Okay, this is where it all starts to sound really weird. Mind you, it's no weirder than waking up in a castle with no memory of who you are or how you got there. True?*

She smiled as some of the missing pieces of the puzzle fell into place. If Thomas was her real 'father', why hadn't he spent time sitting with her and helping her to regain her memory? And why had Iridia, the only other person who might be able to help her, been banned from visiting her?

Okay, so she just needed to open her mind and believe

that anything was possible. She didn't even understand where her preconceived ideas of what *wasn't* possible came from. Something about this Jayce, and his ability to be inside her head, screamed at her to trust him. So she would!

Sounds like you're almost ready to hear the truth. Where would you like me to start?

Ummm... where and when we met, I think. But if you're going to use images, can you please remember to replace the red-head's image with mine. Something about seeing you with her does my head in.

Jayce chuckled, his sensual tones doing weird things to her stomach. *Make yourself comfortable. This may take a while...*

Jayce's voice, interspersed with some incredibly vivid images, spent the next hour replaying the last three weeks of their lives. While the whole story sounded utterly fantastical and unbelievable, some deep-seated sense told her it was all true. Dragons, witches, magic... suddenly it all seemed possible.

Jayce finished his tale and fell silent. He was waiting for her reaction.

Oh, what the hell... what did she have to lose? Anything was better than continuing to live in this disjointed limbo.

Okay, so now I understand the problem, do you by any chance have a solution?

Jayce's breath came out in a loud whoosh, as if he'd been holding it while waiting for her answer. *Well, your mother believes if we cast the spell together, we should be able to restore your memory.*

Right... so how do we do that?

Jayce chuckled again. *You're sounding more like my Ellie every minute. Hang on a sec while I speak to Yvette.*

Ellie chewed on her lip while she waited for Jayce's voice to come back. Without him there to calm her nerves, the doubts began to creep in. What if this really was all in her imagination? She believed herself to be in love with some face from a vision and a voice in her head. What if *she* changed the girl in the images? That was far more believable than some magician casting a spell on her to change the way she looked and erase her memories. Maybe she should...

Elle? Don't fall apart on me now babe. I know you're scared, but you need to trust me just a little longer. I'm one of the good guys, and I'm telling the truth. Besides, if this is all in your imagination, then what have you got to lose? The spell won't work, and my voice will be gone. Come on sweetheart. I miss you so much...

Ellie smiled. There it was again. That damned caressing the mind thing. She didn't think she'd ever be able to say no to that. Jayce's sexy voice chuckled. Damn him... some thoughts were private!

Okay, you win. But stop listening to my every thought. What do I need to do?

That's my girl. Right, the words of the spell are restituet memoria. Oh, and touch your head while you're saying them.

Sorry? Sounds like gobbledegook to me. So if this all turned out to be a product of her overactive imagination, at least she knew she had the makings of a great story-teller. And she would *not* think about the sexy chuckle following those thoughts.

Just repeat the words after me.

She sighed and put her hand up to the side of her head. Jayce said the first word, and she congratulated herself on how well she copied his pronunciation. Then she repeated the rest and held her breath, waiting for something to happen. Not sure what to expect, her heart sunk when nothing changed.

Jayce... I don't think it worked. Her eyes filled with tears, and she swallowed the sob rising in her throat. *I don't feel any different. Are you even still there? Or is this where your voice disappears forever, and I go back to reality?*

She jumped when Jayce's angry growl rumbled in her head. This guy seriously needed to get a handle on his emotions. And then the frustrated but gentle voice came back. *I'm sorry Elle. I'm still here. I don't know why it didn't work. Give me a minute... okay?*

Ellie tried to push down the fear rising into her chest. So, 'the spell', or whatever the hell the gobbledegook really was, didn't work. But Jayce's voice was still in her head. So what now? Jayce's anger and frustration filled her mind. What if she had it all wrong, and *he* was the dangerous one?

She froze as she realised she was *feeling* Jayce's emotions, not just hearing his words. Whatever was happening where he was, the anger dissipated, to be replaced with longing and pain. And suddenly she under-stood. His emotional state was caused by his love and worry for her. A warm fuzzy feeling seeped into her heart. She wanted her life with this man back... *now!*

I'm not sure if it will make any difference, but your mother is going to try and help. The three of us did this once before and it worked, although we were standing together holding hands at the time. But it's worth a try. If we all say the words at the same time, it might be enough. So we'll just have to hope and pray...

Ellie's heart raced, her hand shaking as she lifted it to her head. *Okay, ready when you are. But after this...*

Yeah, I know. Trust me one more time. After three. One, two, three...

As the last word left her mouth, Ellie's stomach lurched, and the room began to spin. She closed her eyes and slipped into the darkness.

CHAPTER ELEVEN

Jayce

*J*ayce raked his hands through his hair, his head still pounding from the energy required to help Ellie break the memory spell. That had been almost half an hour ago, and Ellie's continuing silence was driving him insane. His dragon screamed to be released. What had they done to her?

What if the spell had severed the link between them somehow? He told her if the spell didn't work his voice would disappear from her head. Did she think he'd deserted her? The horrible possibilities tumbled relentlessly through his mind, each one worse than the last.

"Something's wrong. It's been too long. Damnit, I'm not waiting any longer. I need to go—"

Don't even think about it. Jayce went weak at the knees with relief. Ellie's beautiful voice was back in his head.

Well, maybe a bit more bossy than beautiful, but it was still her.

Jayce, I'm fine. I must have passed out after the spell. But I remember everything, so you can stop tearing your hair out. I'm about to teleport out of here now.

Jayce sprung up from the lounge and punched the air. "Yes! Yvette, Jasper... the spell worked! Ellie's back."

Wait... where do I go? Jayce? I don't even know where you are?

Damn it, I forgot you'd never been to the dragon realm. Ummm... let me think. It needs to be somewhere you've been... Got it! How about we meet you back at our room in the hotel?

Awesome... can't wait to see you.

Jayce turned to Yvette and Jasper with a huge grin. "I forgot she's never been here before. She's gonna teleport back to the hotel. Best we be on our way too."

Jayce... wait! He froze at the terror in Ellie's voice. *It's not working... I can't teleport!*

Jayce sucked in a breath and clamped down on his own emotions. Ellie needed him to stay calm and focused, but the fear in her voice made his heart ache.

It's okay babe... don't panic. Thomas must've done something to your magic. I'm sure Yvette will think of something.

Jayce looked at Yvette in desperation. "She can't teleport. What's with that?"

"I was afraid of this. How else would someone be strong enough to take her in the first place? Someone's used dark magic to bind Ellie's magic."

"So how did we restore her memory? Didn't she need to use magic to do that?"

"I can't explain it either, Jayce. The only thing I can think of, is that you reached her magic through your bond. The binding must only stop *her* accessing her magic. But a dark magic spell is a whole other story. Ellie can't reach her own magic by herself. And I can't help her without touching her."

"So what the hell are we supposed to do now? The last thing we need is for Thomas to suspect she has her memory back."

J-Jayce... Ellie's voice shook. *S-someone's at the door. It'll be him... Jayce, what do I do? What if he realises something's different?*

Jayce put his hand up and cut Yvette and Jasper off. He needed to concentrate on helping Ellie.

Elle... stay calm. I'll be with you the whole time. Just try to act the same as the last time you spoke to him.

I'll try. Although the last time I spoke to him, I didn't want to slam him up against a wall and rip him apart.

Jayce chuckled. *Welcome back sweetheart...*

Ahhh Eleanor. I'm pleased to see some colour back in your cheeks. Must be the fresh air. Still no memories? The sound of Thomas' voice in Ellie's head was like fingernails on a blackboard. With a huge effort, he reined in his emotions and concentrated on keeping Ellie calm.

No... nothing yet, Ellie replied cautiously.

Avoid eye contact with him Elle. Tell him your head is aching or something.

I... I think I might spend the rest of the day in bed. The headaches seem to come and go.

Excellent idea. Thomas' smug, oily voice was in her

head again. *I have some Council business to attend to. Shouldn't take too long, and then perhaps we can dine together tonight?*

That would be lovely.

Sleep well dear, and I'll see you tonight. I'm looking forward to us spending some time getting re-acquainted.

Jayce waited until he heard the door close behind Thomas before he released his breath. He wanted Ellie to have dinner with him? Seriously? Probably so he could fill her supposedly empty mind with lies.

Jayce? We need to do something. I can't sit down for a 'pleasant dinner' with Thomas. Even when I had no memories, the man made my skin crawl. He'll be onto me the first time I meet his eyes.

Jasper and Yvette watched him with worried frowns. Of course. They had no idea what was happening. He needed to tell them about the latest development. And think about what the hell to do next.

Okay... hang on a sec. I need to tell Yvette and Jasper what's going on.

"Thomas paid Ellie a visit," Jayce growled out loud. "You should've heard him. Calling her 'dear' and inviting her to a 'cosy dinner'."

Yvette's eyes widened, her face so pale Jayce worried she might faint. "But Ellie knows who he is now. She'll never be able to keep—"

"Exactly. Ellie said the same thing. But the good news is—Thomas is going out for a while. So I can just fly in and—"

"No way Jayce. You'd be flying into a trap. But now

we're sure Thomas has gone out, I can teleport into her room and bring her back." She chewed her lip and paced back and forward. "I'll need Ellie to describe everything about the room, and where in the castle she is."

Jayce groaned. Yvette's plan made much more sense. But it was killing him standing around and doing nothing. *He* wanted to be the one to rescue her, dammit. But then, if he got caught, they'd lose all hope of getting Ellie out. And Thomas would have no more reason to keep her alive.

Jayce, mum's right. No-one will see her coming. Please... I don't care how it happens, I just need to be out of here before Thomas gets back.

The terror in Ellie's voice brought him to his senses. He needed to stop worrying about what *he* wanted and focus on getting Elle away from Thomas. *Who* did it, wasn't the issue.

I'm sorry babe. You're both right. So can you describe the room to me, and I'll try to work out where you are?

Ellie rattled off a detailed description of the room and the view from her window. Jayce recognised it immediately. Thomas had her in the 'guest wing'. Though he had always wondered why it was called that, when visitors never stayed over at the castle. Jayce and his best friend, Rhett, had dubbed it the 'ghost wing' when they were kids. They'd used it as their 'secret hideout' from Thomas' violent mood swings.

"Yvette... I know where she is! I'll draw you a map and you can be in and out in no time."

Hang in there, sweetheart... Yvette is coming.

Jayce drew a quick sketch of the layout of the castle, highlighting the 'guest wing' and Ellie's room. Yvette studied the map, nodding when she had a clear picture in her head.

"This will be like taking candy from a baby, as they say." She smiled and winked at Jayce. "Be right back."

Jayce held his breath and sent a silent prayer to the Stars. He jumped when, instead of vanishing, Yvette staggered backwards as if she'd been punched.

"What the hell...?" Jasper and Jayce ran to Yvette, who sat on the ground holding her head.

Jayce... Where's Yvette? What's going on?

Jayce groaned. *She's still here, but I've no idea why. Hang on...*

"Woah, that was weird! The castle must be warded. So even if Ellie's powers were intact, she still couldn't teleport anywhere."

So what are we gonna do now?

Damnit Elle, I don't know. But if we don't think of a solution soon, I'm coming to get you!

Ellie

ELLIE FLOPPED down on the bed, pulled her pillow over her face, and screamed her frustration. Thomas could be back any minute, and she refused to even contemplate the idea of having dinner with him. The thought of trying to keep up the humble idiot act, while sitting opposite him, made her want to throw up. Thomas would know as soon as she made eye contact that her memories were back, and then all hell would break loose.

Okay, time to stop thinking like *Eleanor* and get her act together. She threw the pillow back on the bed and jumped to her feet, chewing her thumb nail as she paced the floor.

Think Ellie! There's gotta be another way out. She stopped pacing and slapped her forehead. What the hell was she doing, whinging and griping about someone coming to get her out of here? Poor Jayce. She'd only been living with the reality of her situation for hours... Jayce had been going through this for days.

She needed to stop acting like the stupid 'damsel-in-distress' Jayce already considered her and prove him wrong. And sitting here quivering in her boots and expecting everyone else to come up with solutions definitely wasn't going to do that. This was *her* problem, and she would find a way out herself.

Okay, so how? She couldn't exactly just walk out of the place. She had no idea where she was or where to go. But... maybe...? An idea began to take shape in her head.

Jayce... I'm so sorry I've been snapping and snarling ever since I got my memory back. I know you're doing everything you can.

You don't have anything to be sorry for. I'm the one who

should be apologising. Damnit, I don't care what anyone says... I'm coming—

NO! Jayce you can't! Thomas will be waiting for you.

I don't give a damn. I have to do something—

Well... I've been thinking. What about your mother? Couldn't she fly me out of here? Surely she's free to leave the castle whenever she wants?

Elle, that's brilliant! Except... Jayce groaned, and Ellie pictured him running his hands through his hair as he always did when he was frustrated. *Good luck persuading her to take the risk of upsetting Thomas. The poor woman is terrified of him.*

What if I offered to take her back with us to the mortal world? I'll explain to her that we can protect her. Plus, she would be with you again.

I honestly think she'll be too frightened to help you. But I guess it's worth a try. Do you think you can find her?

She'll probably be hiding somewhere. Thomas told her to stay away from me because she might 'upset' me. Yeah right. More like he didn't want her to spill any of his secrets.

Okay, I can give you directions to her rooms. That's more than likely where she'll be holed up.

I'm not sure if he left someone guarding my door. Guess we'll soon find out, eh?

Ellie held her breath as she slowly opened the door. The hallway looked deserted. She let the breath out in a loud *whoosh*. Finally, something was going right for a change.

All clear. Where to now?

She squared her shoulders and walked through the

silent castle, Jayce's voice in her head directing her as she went. She broke out in a sweat, her nerves buzzing like electrical wires, terrified someone would reach out and drag her back to her room.

Deep breaths Elle... you're almost there. Jayce's soothing voice was all that kept her putting one foot in front of the other. Her footsteps seemed to echo in the silence as she crept through the massive castle.

What felt like hours - but was probably closer to five minutes - later, she stood outside what she hoped was Iridia's door. She knocked and waited, her legs shaking as scenarios of being caught and trying to explain why she was there ran through her head.

The door opened, and Iridia's face paled. "Please, can I come in? I'm sorry. I know you're not supposed to talk to me. But I really need your help."

The woman hesitated, and finally nodded, opening the door wide enough for Ellie to enter. As soon as Ellie slipped inside, Iridia closed the door and waved her towards a well-worn lounge. The older woman sat down opposite her and sighed.

"I'm sorry, but I can't help you. Thomas would—" Iridia shuddered and closed her eyes.

"Iridia... did he tell you who I am? Or why I'm here in the castle?"

Iridia opened her eyes and covered her mouth, her eyes filling with tears as she shook her head. "No, but I'm afraid it wouldn't make any difference if he did. Thomas would kill me if I interfered in his business."

Ellie took a deep breath and smiled. "What if it was to help Jayce?"

Iridia paled at the mention of her son's name. "What? You know my Jayce? Is he alright?"

Ellie moved to sit beside her, reaching for her hand. "He's fine, or at least he was a few minutes ago, when I last spoke to him."

"How did you...? Where is he?

"It's a long story. He's at a castle nearby. Someone called Amos' place?"

"But Amos is in league with Thomas. He shouldn't be anywhere near here. Please... you need to tell him to leave." The tears were now pouring down Iridia's face. No matter what else happened, Ellie decided she was getting the poor woman out of this place.

"Iridia, we don't have much time, and I have a lot to tell you about Jayce. Please just listen, and then you can decide whether you want to help us."

Iridia nodded, and Ellie launched into an edited version of what had been going on. The woman's eyes grew wider and wider as she spoke. By the time Ellie reached the part where Jayce threatened to fly in and save her, she knew Iridia would help her.

"I can't say I'm surprised at the atrocities Thomas is capable of, but I will die before I let him hurt Jayce. Hurry, we need to go... NOW."

Jayce? Did you hear all that? We'll be there soon...

She waited for Jayce's reply as Iridia moved toward the wall. For a second, she thought Iridia had lost all sense of direction, until the woman opened a door Ellie hadn't even noticed was there.

Seeing the surprise on Ellie's face, Iridia almost smiled. "This is a shortcut to the enclosed courtyard where we met. Hurry, I want to be long gone before Thomas gets home."

As Ellie crossed the room and entered the concealed doorway, Jayce's voice was back in her head. *Thank you, beautiful girl for convincing her to leave him. I love you.* His voice broke, and her heart ached. *Tell my mother we'll be waiting in the courtyard for you.*

CHAPTER TWELVE

Jayce

*H*earing Ellie's voice inside his head was the only thing keeping Jayce from falling apart. She kept up a running commentary as she followed Iridia down the stairs leading to the courtyard.

He shivered at her terror when Iridia pushed open the door to step outside, images of being caught and dragged back inside the castle playing through Ellie's mind.

Elle, stop imagining the worst. You're gonna give me a heart attack.

Oops, sorry. Forgot you were in my head too. I'll try to keep the dramatic thoughts to a minimum.

Ellie's excitement washed over him as Iridia released her dragon, the thought of escaping becoming a reality. Jayce paced the courtyard at Amos' castle, knowing it could all fall to pieces any minute.

2

CHAPTER TWELVE

Jayce

*H*earing Ellie's voice inside his head was the only thing keeping Jayce from falling apart. She kept up a running commentary as she followed Iridia down the stairs leading to the courtyard.

He shivered at her terror when Iridia pushed open the door to step outside, images of being caught and dragged back inside the castle playing through Ellie's mind.

Elle, stop imagining the worst. You're gonna give me a heart attack.

Oops, sorry. Forgot you were in my head too. I'll try to keep the dramatic thoughts to a minimum.

Ellie's excitement washed over him as Iridia released her dragon, the thought of escaping becoming a reality. Jayce paced the courtyard at Amos' castle, knowing it could all fall to pieces any minute.

88

Elle, you need to tell my mother how you use my tail—

Yeah, yeah. I'm onto it, she replied, quickly explaining the concept to Iridia. Seconds later, she started to grumble, and Jayce pictured her scrambling across Iridia's back. Jayce laughed when he realised what she'd been grumbling about. She hated flying without her harness. His Ellie was definitely back.

Okay, we're on our way. Please Stars we make it before anyone notices we're missing.

Jayce sagged with relief and turned to Jasper and Yvette. "They're on their way."

Yvette's eyes filled with tears as Jasper wrapped an arm around her shoulders. As if by mutual agreement, they waited in silence, all eyes focused on the skies above them.

Jayce's heart hammered in his chest as he tried not to imagine all the things that could go wrong before they were safe.

Now who's being the dramatic one? Ellie's voice was barely a whisper in his mind. He smiled as he pictured her clinging to his mother's neck, her nerves stretched to breaking point.

The distance between the two castles was short, but it felt like hours before his mother's beautiful silver dragon came into sight.

Jayce's eyes filled with tears. *I can see you... you're almost here.*

Jasper and Yvette stood on either side of him as Iridia landed smoothly in the courtyard. Ellie released her hold on Iridia's neck, up and running across the dragon's broad back within seconds.

He chuckled at the impatient expression on her face. She had no intention of waiting for Iridia to bring her tail around. Filled with the same impatience, he ran to catch her as she dived into his arms.

The world around them ceased to exist. Jayce's heart leapt as their lips met, the kiss like air to a drowning man. He vowed he would never let her out of his sight again.

I will need to go to the bathroom sometimes. He laughed, her soft husky voice intoxicating.

We'll discuss that later.

Yvette tapped him on the shoulder, and they reluctantly drew apart. "Yeah, yeah I know. Time to go."

"Actually, I was going to say you should at least both say hello to your mothers." Yvette tried to maintain a stern look despite her tear-filled eyes and twitching smile.

Jayce tore himself away from Ellie and turned to his mother. He wrapped his arms around her, gently pulling her emaciated body into a hug. She was so wasted away he hardly recognised her. Hatred for the man responsible for her condition flared up inside him.

"Oh Jayce, I'm so happy you're safe." She smiled up into his eyes. "Well, I'm going to assume you're my son, since Ellie almost broke her neck trying to reach you. But why do you look like that grovelling worm Riley King? You don't even smell like you."

Jayce chuckled. "Hello mama... long story. But forget about me... this is about you. You're a hero. I am so proud of you for having the courage to finally leave that animal. And thank you so much for bringing my Elle back to me."

He smiled as Ellie hugged her mother, both laughing and crying at the same time.

"Damnit, how come every time we see each other we're wearing someone else's bodies?" Ellie mumbled through the tears.

Yvette smiled and shrugged. "Desperate times call for desperate measures. Come on, let's go home. I must've been hanging around Jayce too long. I have a sudden urge to shed this creepy skin."

Jayce laughed, sobering at the sight of Jasper standing alone watching the family reunions. His heart went out to the old man. Losing his only son, daughter-in-law and unborn grandchild years ago must have almost killed him. Ellie picked up on his thoughts and moved toward the old dragon.

"You may look like Amos, but it's you, isn't it Jasper?"

A tender smile split the older man's face, and he enclosed Ellie in a warm hug. "Great to have you back girl. We missed you more than you can possibly imagine."

Yvette joined them, smiling as she brushed her tears away with a smile. "Yeah, what he said. Now, how about we get out of here before we receive any unwanted visitors?"

Everyone nodded, and Jayce and his mother completed their circle. He squeezed her hand and looked into her worried eyes. "Yvette is going to teleport us back to the mortal world. You might want to close your eyes and count to three. The first time can be a bit of a head spin. I love you mama... and thank you, a thousand times over."

Instantly, the cobbled courtyard fell away beneath their feet, and then they were standing in Ellie and Jayce's room. Isabel's face lit up as she raced across the room and into Jasper's waiting arms.

"Oh Stars... I swear this has been the longest day of my life. Ellie! Oh, honey it's so good to see you." Releasing Jasper, she enveloped Ellie in a huge hug. Wiping the tears from her face, she looked around at them all. "So... coffee for... six?" Her eyes fell on Iridia, and her jaw dropped. "Dia? Is that really you?"

All eyes turned to the two women staring at each other in shock.

"Izzy?" Iridia said, a smile on her face

"Don't tell me you two know each other?" Jayce said, his arm tightly wrapped around Ellie's waist.

"We grew up together. But we lost touch and haven't seen one another in... what? Twenty years?" Isabel said, hugging the other woman.

Yvette smiled, looking at Jasper, Isabel and Iridia with a wicked grin. "So, I was thinking. How about we head to Jasper and Isabel's room for an hour or so and give these two some time to themselves?"

"Mum... could you at least be a little more subtle about it," Ellie groaned, the adorable blush spreading up her neck making Jayce want to push them all out the door.

Yvette laughed as she herded them all out. "Like I said

one hour!" She winked as she pulled the door closed behind them.

Ellie turned and reached up to place her hands on Jayce's face. "Can you ever forgive me? I'm so sorry I went to the aunts' without—"

Jayce's lips ended her apology before she could finish the sentence. He bent down and picked her up, cradling her against his chest. His fears of never again being able to hold her, or gaze into her beautiful emerald eyes, were buried in the past. Apologies would be nothing more than a waste of their precious time alone together.

Ellie

ELLIE CURSED as the phone rang beside her. She slipped out of Jayce's arms and answered, still half asleep.

"Hello..."

"Ellie, we'll be there in five minutes." Ellie's eyes flew open at her mother's voice.

"No worries. See you soon." She hung up and squealed, pulling Jayce out of bed. "They'll be here in five minutes. Quick, help me make the bed."

Jayce chuckled. "Don't you think it might be more important to be wearing *clothes* when they get here?"

Ellie cracked up laughing at the wicked glint in his

eyes. "Good point. Thank the Stars one of us is thinking clearly."

She grabbed her clothes and ran for the bathroom. "So, if you have time after you're dressed, can you please make the bed?" She grinned at the 'long suffering' expression on his face as she closed the door. *Damn, it was good to be home.*

About to step into the shower, she caught sight of herself in the mirror. She stared at the black haired, brown-eyed girl reflected back at her. Thomas had certainly been thorough. Pity he underestimated the strength of the telepathic bond between her and Jayce. She shook her head and slid under the stream of hot water, smiling at the thought of Thomas' reaction when he discovered not only her gone, but his wife as well.

She shivered at the memory of Thomas' smugness when she agreed to have dinner with him. How Jayce had lived with the man for so long, and turned out his polar opposite, was beyond her. Jayce had never even considered straying from the path of his own destiny, no matter what his father had made him endure.

Then there was Iridia. Ellie remembered Jayce telling them how his father beat his mother if Jayce stepped out of line. The man really was a monster and had proven himself a fierce and bitter enemy.

Bring. It. On, Ellie thought, washing away the last traces of her time in the enemy's castle. *I'll be ready for you this time!*

Suddenly aware of how much time had passed, she dived out of the shower, towelled herself dry and threw on her clothes. When she came out of the bathroom, she found the bed already made. And the delicious aroma wafting in from the lounge room told her Jayce had also made coffee. *Wow! All that and domesticated too. What more could a girl want.*

She skipped into the loungeroom and climbed into his lap. "I love you. Thank you for being you."

Jayce cupped her face in his hands, his thumbs brushing against the corner of her lips. "I love you too beautiful girl."

Ellie cringed at the loud knocking on the door. She wanted to stay wrapped up in this warm cocoon forever. The whole 'save the world' thing was seriously over-rated.

Jayce's arms tightened as he read her thoughts. Then he, too, sighed, kissed the top of her head, and moved her to the lounge beside him. "I know babe. But while-ever Thomas is out there, we'll never have any peace."

Ellie groaned as Jayce got to his feet and went to open the door. *Fine, but when this is all over...*

He threw her a sultry grin as he opened the door. *You better believe it...*

Ellie suppressed a giggle as he waved their visitors into the room, relieved to see Yvette and Jasper's glamours gone. She jumped up and grabbed her mother's hand, shuddering as she remembered her own reflection earlier.

"So, it must be my turn to look normal again. I am so over seeing Eleanor in the mirror.

"That makes two of us. Come on, let's do this." Yvette draped her arm around Ellie's shoulder and headed for the bedroom. Ellie blushed as they entered the room, imagining her mother's face had she seen it five minutes earlier. She sent a message to Jayce, thanking him for making the bed and straightening up the mess.

"Right then," Yvette said with a smile. "Before we deal with the glamour, I think we should find out what's going on with your magic."

Ellie's skin tingled as Yvette cast the spell to detect the use of dark magic, her eyes narrowing as her mother growled at whatever she found.

"Just as I thought. Dark magic. Binding someone's magic is not something that can be done with regular magic. Did Thomas cast the spell?"

"No. The guy in the aunts' kitchen who took me to Thomas did it. I remember being hit by incredible pain and nausea as soon as I stepped into the room."

"So he's working with others who are using dark magic. Normally I would take this straight to the Witch Council, but who knows how many of them he's corrupted. I'm sorry honey, but you should probably expect the same reaction as last time. Maybe we should do this in the bathroom."

Ellie nodded and followed her mother into the bathroom, where she perched on the edge of the bathtub and closed her eyes. She gritted her teeth, bracing herself for a re-run of the pain she experienced the last time this spell was cast. Not something she was looking forward to repeating.

Yvette cast the spell, and the same wave of pain and nausea hit her like a freight train. She controlled the desire to empty her stomach, being prepared for the horrific sensations this time. She breathed through the pain, relieved to find the hollow ache in her stomach gone. She finally felt whole again.

"Are you okay honey?"

Ellie opened her eyes and smiled up at her mother. "You have no idea. It feels fantastic. I can't even begin to describe how horrible it felt before. Thank you so much."

Yvette sighed. "Thank the Stars. I didn't want to worry you, but I was terrified my magic wouldn't be powerful enough to break the spell. Okay, now let's get rid of Eleanor so I can hug my *real* daughter."

Yvette quickly cast the spell to remove the glamour and pulled Ellie into her arms. They turned to the mirror, and Ellie smiled at her reflection. The nightmare was finally over.

They re-entered the lounge room arm in arm, laughing for no particular reason, then stopped at Iridia's sharp intake of breath.

"Oh, my goodness." Iridia's eyes were wide with shock. "I hardly recognised you, Ellie. The real you is even more beautiful than the other one. Ooh, I'm going to have such gorgeous grandchildren."

Ellie blushed scarlet, while everyone else in the room chuckled. She groaned and climbed back into Jayce's lap. He tried to mask the laughter in his eyes as he gave his mother an *almost* stern look. "Goodonya Mama, now you've embarrassed my beautiful fiancé."

"I'm sorry son, but I'm still having trouble taking you seriously when you're wearing Riley's face." Iridia replied, a sparkle in her eyes.

Jayce threw his head back and laughed. "Oh yeah, I forgot about that. Yvette, I'd really appreciate looking like myself again about now too?" Yvette nodded, and Jayce scooped Ellie up and dumped her on her butt beside him. "Stay right there. I just need to dispose of Riley and get Jayce back." He grinned as he planted a kiss on her forehead.

CHAPTER THIRTEEN

Ellie

*I*ridia's eyes lit up as Yvette cast the spell to remove Jayce's glamour. Ellie had forgotten Jayce appeared to everyone else as this person named Riley, and she smiled as his mother jumped up and reached out to hug her son.

She released him and stepped back, holding him at arms' length. "I knew it was you on the inside, but seeing you... well, somehow it makes it all more *real*. I'm so proud of the amazing man you've grown into."

Jayce gave Ellie a long-suffering look over his mother's shoulder, and Iridia let out an embarrassed laugh. "Okay, I won't keep you from Ellie any longer." The older woman turned and winked at Ellie as she sat back down in her own chair, smiling at Jayce's sheepish grin as he dropped back down beside Ellie.

Jasper appeared to have been waiting for the lull in conversation and cleared his throat. "Ummm, I hate to ruin the party, but there's some unfinished business we need to deal with before we start planning our next move." His eyes shifted towards the far corner of the lounge room, and Ellie realised three people lay on the floor asleep.

"O... kay," she said, looking around at the others. "So that's how you made sure they wouldn't make a surprise appearance. Do they know what's been going on?"

Jayce growled and Ellie's eyes flew to his. "Okay, so what don't *I* know?"

Jasper rubbed the back of his neck. "Remember when Amos said the old ones affected by the poison would be left to die? Well, I should have known something wasn't right. The rogues would never sanction the loss of lives resulting from that decision. Thomas orchestrated the whole thing. Amos was simply his puppet. Thomas knew you would risk everything to go to their aid, 'specially if you believed the aunts would die without your help. The man seems to be able to predict how you and Jayce will react in every situation."

Ellie looked down at her hands, shame washing over her at what she put them all through because of her pigheadedness. "I'm so sorry. I had this nightmare the aunts died, and I woke up terrified it had already happened. I thought I was being so careful... even tele-ported to the school and walked to the house in case someone followed me. The guy who grabbed me said he'd been waiting for me. But wait, why would Amos do what

Thomas asked? He's supposed to be the leader of the rebellion. I don't understand."

"You may recall when we first met, I told you the Council were declaring more and more wealthy and respected dragons rogue?" Ellie nodded. "Well, Thomas threatened to declare Amos a rogue, and of course he panicked. Although he's been working for the rebellion, Amos has never been declared a rogue. Which always came in handy when we needed someone inside the dragon realm to garner information. I'm so sorry Ellie. I should never have brought you here. I never dreamed Amos would—"

"None of this is your fault Jasper," Jayce said between gritted teeth. "Thomas figured that if he burned our home, we would eventually come to Amos for refuge. He's been one step ahead of us the whole time."

"So how did you make Amos admit all this?"

Yvette chuckled. "I believe you're familiar with the truth spell? You remember, the one you used on the lecherous old goat who tried to attack you on your trip to Jasper and Isabel's?"

Ellie shivered at the memory of waking up alone in the forest in the presence of a psychopath. "*That's* not something I'm likely to forget in a hurry. Okay, so what do we do with Amos and his two cronies now?"

"I called a meeting of the other leaders of the rebellion for later this evening. They'll decide the fate of these three after hearing all the evidence." A slow smile crept over the old man's face. "Besides, once Thomas learns they were supposedly at Amos' castle when you escaped,

I don't think they'll be welcome in the dragon realm again."

"Sooo... you're telling me they'll be staying there until tonight?" The thought of them being in their room gave her the creeps.

"Well, Yvette can wake them, and we'll take them up to Amos' office later. We also need to discuss the best place to hide while we plan our next move. Thomas knows where we are, and he's going to be hopping mad when he discovers you and Iridia are gone, if he hasn't already."

Jayce growled at the mention of Thomas' name, and Ellie snuggled against him a little closer. She shuddered at the thought of what Thomas would do if he got hold of them.

"From what I've seen, our only hope is to reverse whatever infected the Council members from both realms while they were inside the Aqueous flow. The Lord of the Lake instructed the Aqueous to purge the flow and remove any taint. So, if Thomas managed to place the taint in there, how hard would it be for someone to do the same with a cure?"

Ellie shuddered, staring at Jayce in horror. "Please tell me you're not suggesting we go back to Brevis. The memories of our last visit still give me nightmares."

Jayce squeezed her hand and smiled. "Yeah, I know babe...but we did leave on good terms with the Lord of the Lake. I don't think there'd be too many other people who could say the same."

Jasper held up his hand. "How about we wait and see what the rebellion leaders come up with tonight before we go making any plans? Jayce, I think your mother needs to tell you something important, if the poor woman ever gets a word in."

Jayce raised his eyebrows and turned to his mother. She sat wringing her hands in her lap, a blush creeping up her neck. "Mama... what is it?"

Iridia looked up, tears welling in her eyes. "Oh Jayce, I'm so sorry. You should've been told this a long time ago; but as usual I was too much of a coward to go against Thomas' wishes."

Jayce jumped up from the lounge and crouched down in front of his mother, reaching for her hands. " You're not to blame for anything my father ever said or did. You and I both did what we needed to survive. Now what is this big secret?"

Iridia smiled through her tears. "That's what I've been trying to tell you darling... he's *not* your father. I found out I was pregnant before I married Thomas. Your father, my first husband and the love of my life, died in a hunting accident before you were born."

Jayce looked as though he'd been hit by a stun gun. His mouth opened and closed a few times, but no words came out. He sat down on the floor and shook his head. Ellie was about to jump up and comfort him when he started to laugh.

"Well I'll be damned," he spluttered. "That is, without a doubt, the best news ever. All those years I spent terrified of turning out like him because I shared his DNA. You know what's funny? When we first met Jasper, he said he couldn't understand how someone like me could be related to a monster like him." He looked at Jasper and winked. "Guess you hit the nail right on the head." Then a frown chased all traces of the laughter from his face. "Wait. How did my real father die? Are you sure it was an accident? No suspicious circumstances?"

Iridia shook her head. "Thomas was there, but your father was killed by an arrow from one of the other hunters. Thomas simply brought me the news. I was grieving and alone and pregnant. Thomas offered comfort and understanding. So when he asked me to marry him, I foolishly said yes. I didn't realise he—"

"Don't apologise mama, Ellie and I have seen how he can turn on the charm. His performance as Ellie's supposed 'father' was nauseatingly believable. I just wish I'd been a fly on the wall when he found her missing... and that she took you with her!"

"S-so you're not angry with me?" Iridia said through her tears.

Jayce knelt and wrapped his arms around his mother. "No Mama, of course I'm not. I'm surprised *you* don't hate *me* for what he did to you every time he wanted to punish me. I spent years hating myself for what I put you through."

"I was always glad when he hurt me instead of you. For me, it was the lesser of two evils."

"Well... the nightmare is over. You're safe now, and I promise that monster will never get near you again."

Thomas

THOMAS ARRIVED home from the meeting pleased with his evening's work. The Council members were becoming easier to manipulate every day, as the paranoia and mistrust among them festered and grew. It shouldn't be too long before they started trying to destroy each other, totally unaware they all suffered from the same irrational fear of being murdered in their sleep. The taint he planted in the Aqueous flow had done his work for him.

Thomas strolled into his study to pour himself a well-deserved drink, surprised to find himself looking forward to sitting down to dinner with his newly acquired 'daughter'. A plan had slowly come together while he sat through his boring business meeting.

He would tell the girl the 'sad tale' of 'her brother' who'd betrayed both his family and his own people. Building the girl's hatred against Jayce would be the icing on the cake. It would be yet another unpleasant surprise for the whelp to deal with when he charged in on his 'white horse' to rescue his 'love'. And then the young fool would be carted off and executed.

Thomas shivered with pleasure at the thought of all his long-term goals coming to fruition at last. Admittedly, Jayce and Ellie's interference in his planned eradication of the mortal world had been a blow. Still, it served its purpose in drawing them out and allowing him to test their ability. Together, they had proven a formidable enemy, reinforcing his decision to eliminate one of them.

It had been a stroke of genius on his part to come up with the idea of stealing the morwitch. Since she now lacked any predetermined ideas of who or what she was, she would be putty in his hands. He would soon mould her into his willing slave. Once the Council disposed of Jayce, Thomas would convince her it was her duty as his daughter to bond with *him* as her familiar. With their combined power, they would be unstoppable.

He threw down the last of his drink and headed toward the guest wing to fetch 'Eleanor' for dinner. He knocked and entered, the smile freezing on his face as he found the room empty. The girl was nowhere to be seen. Where could she...? Iridia. He growled and turned toward his wife's rooms, his fists tightly clenched as he strode swiftly down the hallway. What if the witch knew the truth? If Iridia had ruined his plans he would...

Thomas reefed open the door to Iridia's room and yelled for her to come to him. He paced the small sitting room, furious at how long the woman kept him waiting.

Wait. Why would her private door to the courtyard be open? Of course. He pictured them sitting together having a pleasant little tête-à-tête. Even after he ordered her not to leave her rooms? She would pay dearly for her insolent behaviour.

He roared as he stormed down the stairs, imagining the two of them cowering in fear at his imminent arrival.

He cursed himself for taking Ellie's guard to the meeting, but he would never consider attending a meeting without his own personal protector. Besides, the girl seemed so weak and insipid—hardly a flight risk. Unless... no, that was impossible. He burst out into the courtyard only to find it deserted. There was no sign of Iridia or the morwitch! *What the hell...?*

CHAPTER FOURTEEN

Jayce

*J*ayce rolled onto his back and stared up at the ceiling. Wide-awake, he'd been struggling for hours against the urge to release his dragon and go after the man intent on destroying everyone Jayce knew and loved. His mother might believe Thomas' role as an innocent bystander at the death of his real father, but Jayce's mind spun with suspicion.

Thomas was there when the 'accident' happened, wielded magic no-one was aware of, and had walked away with the dead man's wife, reputation and possessions. Thomas had definitely been involved somehow.

Whatever! As far as he was concerned, the solution was simple. Thomas needed to die, and Jayce wanted to be the one to kill him. Thomas and all his followers deserved to burn in hell, and Jayce would be more than happy to be the one to put them there. A driving need for vengeance clawed at his insides.

Wait. Since when was he so obsessed with killing? He remembered his horror at the thought of having to kill the bounty hunter who'd tried to take Ellie only weeks ago. He shrugged... people change.

Together, he and Ellie held the power to destroy Thomas. Well, Ellie did—with his help. He growled in frustration. Just another thing that made his blood boil. Why did Ellie hold all the power? She alone got to decide when and where to use the magic, while he played the role of the magicless sidekick. Everything would be fine if he possessed his own magic.

Knowing he wouldn't be sleeping anytime soon, he climbed out of bed and went out on the balcony, sucking the fresh air into his lungs. After a few deep breaths, the anger began to fade.

Where did all that come from anyway? Ever since Ellie was taken away from him, the bouts of rage had been coming on more and more often. They hadn't used their power together for ages, not like in the beginning. Could his mind be starting to crave the use of the magic?

Nausea washed over him as the words hit home. Stars... was he seriously becoming an addict? He stiffened as a shuffling sound alerted him to Ellie's arrival.

"Hey babe... you okay?"

Jayce groaned and ran his hands through his hair. "Been awake long?"

"Long enough to hear what's been going on inside

your head. Jayce, I'm scared. This can't be normal. We need to tell someone what's happening."

"Don't stress. I can control it. Besides, who are we gonna talk to? Your mother?" He sniffed in disdain at the idea.

Ellie's eyes widened at his angry retort. "Why not? Or Jasper? How long has this been going on?

"Ever since you disappeared. I was terrified I'd never find you, and I put the feelings down to that. But something is definitely off. The anger comes in waves, and they seem to be getting closer together."

Ellie stepped up and placed her hands on either side of his face. "Are you *really* angry with me for being the one who controls the magic? Because I would give it all to you in a heartbeat if I could."

Jayce sighed and pulled her against him. "Of course I'm not angry with you. I love you. I honestly wish I knew where these thoughts were coming from." He kissed the top of her head and shuddered. "Maybe you're right. We *should* tell someone. But let's wait 'til the morning. My head is pounding."

Ellie's worried eyes searched his, as if she would somehow find the answers he couldn't give her. "Fine. But promise me we'll tell them about this tomorrow?"

Jayce chuckled as he swept her up into his arms and held her against his chest. "Alright Miss Worry-Wort, I promise. Now let's go back to bed!"

Ellie giggled and wrapped her arms around his neck. "If you insist, Mr Bossy-Boots."

Ellie

ELLIE WOKE to find Jayce's side of the bed empty. She stretched and sniffed the air, hoping his absence meant coffee would be waiting. But no delicious aroma wafted in from the kitchen. Remembering their conversation from the previous night, she scrambled out of bed to go find him.

Jayce sat on the lounge with his face in his hands.

"Hey babe... How long you been up?"

Jayce lifted his head, his eyes bloodshot and filled with anger. "All night... couldn't sleep," he said through gritted teeth.

"Okay, I'm calling my mother. This is ridiculous. You've been going through this all night? Why didn't you wake me?"

Jayce shrugged and dropped his face back into his hands. "I'm scared I've developed some form of addiction. I want the magic so bad my own thoughts are driving me insane."

Ellie ran to the phone, dialled Jasper's room, where Yvette and Iridia had stayed last night, and told her she needed her to come straight away. Yvette appeared beside her before she could even hang up.

"What's wrong? Are you alright?" Yvette asked.

"I'm fine, this is about Jayce. Come sit down and we'll tell you what's been going on."

Ellie curled up on the lounge next to Jayce, telling Yvette about his angry thoughts.

Yvette frowned and chewed on her lip as she listened. "This is not good. I've never heard or read about anything like this before. But then, nothing you two experience is ever normal. I can't even think of anyone who might be able to help."

Ellie sat up in excitement. "What about the Tree of Life? Remember when we healed Her, She said something about our intervention being 'foreseen by the Stars'? She might know what we're supposed to do.

Hope flared in Jayce's eyes, making her heart ache. "It's worth a try. The Tree's been around longer than any other living being."

"I'm going to call the others first. Jasper may know something we don't. We planned to sit down this morning and discuss what went on at the meeting last night. I guess that can wait."

As Yvette rose to move toward the phone, Jayce spoke through gritted teeth. "Just don't take too long. I'm not sure how much longer I can keep the anger and the urges under control."

Yvette nodded and punched in the number for Jasper and Isabel's room. Ellie couldn't make out the words, but the conversation didn't last long. They sat in tense silence until the knock came at the door. Yvette hurried to answer it and waved their friends inside.

Jasper walked up and put a hand on Jayce's shoulder. "Hey son... you wanna tell us what's going on?"

Jayce brushed Jasper's hand away and jumped to his feet. He ran his hands through his hair and paced as he explained about the thoughts going through his head. "It only started after Ellie disappeared. Almost as if not being around her magic caused a chain reaction. And now the rage is like a germ, spreading at a rate of knots."

Jasper scratched his head and sighed. "I'm sorry son, I don't know how to help you. You're the only dragon I ever met who had access to magic. It's possible the power is corrupting you somehow."

Jayce froze and went white as a ghost. "Stars Jasper, I think you're right. That would explain what happened to Thomas. He was born with the magic already in his blood. What if, when he started to use it, the corruption just took over?"

Ellie's stomach heaved. "Oh. My. Stars. What if that's why the bond was outlawed? No wonder the Councils were frightened of the other couple who bonded. But why didn't they tell anyone? And how do we stop it?"

Jasper shook his head. "I wish I knew. So, we need to find someone who can help as soon as possible. Yvette, is there a spell you can cast on Jayce to slow the spread of whatever this is? Or do you think letting him use some magic might help?" He threw his hands in the air. "There has to be something we can do?"

"Ellie suggested we go visit the Tree of Life, and I'm starting to think that may be our only option. There's no telling whether using the magic again will make it better or worse."

"We'll start with something easy. Umm, fetching is relatively simple, and we've done that plenty of times." Ellie stood and slipped her arms around Jayce's waist. "What do you think babe?"

Jayce groaned. "I'm the last person you should ask. But I'm open to suggestions."

"Okay, let's try it then. How about we fetch something of yours from the bedroom? See how that makes you feel?"

Jayce nodded and they both closed their eyes. Ellie shuddered as the magic raged through her. She opened her eyes, panic racing through her at the speed they were retrieving the clothes. "Ummm Jayce... I think we can stop now. Are you okay?"

Jayce's eyes snapped open, barely controlled rage burning in their fiery depths. Before she could move, he slumped to the floor, unconscious. "What the—?"

Yvette looked at Ellie through pain-filled eyes. "I'm sorry honey. I couldn't risk him hurting you. I cast a sleeping spell on him when I saw the angry glow in his eyes. He would never forgive himself if he hurt you, and I think the corruption is spreading faster than he can control it."

Ellie dropped down beside him, tears flowing as she pulled Jayce's head up on her lap. "What are we gonna do? How do we stop it?"

The silence in the room made her want to scream in

frustration. Why wasn't anyone coming up with answers? Somebody needed to do something! Now!

"Fine... I'm going to talk to the Tree. I refuse to sit around here and let Jayce go insane."

CHAPTER FIFTEEN

Ellie

*T*he ground fell away and Ellie stood outside the entrance to the Tree of Life's sanctuary. She groaned as the hot, sticky air of the Amazon jungle enveloped her. Ewww... she'd forgotten about that. Sighing, she tied her hair back into a knot and tried to get her bearings. Damnit. How was she supposed to contact the Tree and ask for access to the sanctuary?

She jumped as Yvette appeared beside her. "You could've waited for me. I would never let you do this alone."

Ellie breathed a sigh of relief and turned to hug her mother. "I'm sorry. I was just so—"

Yvette returned the hug and smiled. "Okay, I'll forgive you just this once. Besides... I probably would've reacted the same way in your shoes."

Ellie nodded, unable to speak past the lump in her

throat. She didn't even want to think about the future if they couldn't find a cure. Surely the Stars wouldn't let this happen to them, after all they'd done. So much for their union being blessed. Didn't take the 'oh-so-powerful-ones' long to desert them.

Shaking off the negative thoughts, she stepped back out of her mother's arms. "So... we never thought to ask the Tree how to get back in if we needed to come back. I didn't expect to ever—"

A crackling sound cut through the silence as the trees marking the entrance to the sanctuary began to move. As they shifted, they revealed a huge set of doors, which slowly creaked open. Ellie and Yvette smiled.

"Guess She knows we're here then," Ellie said, as they stepped through the doors and into paradise. Not a trace of the desolate wilderness they encountered on their previous visits remained.

She grabbed Yvette's hand, strolling across the carpet-like lush green grass, interspersed with a myriad of flowers of every colour, shape and size. The air smelled fresh and clean, sweetened by the intoxicating scent of the various wildlife.

Ellie sighed as they reached the Tree of Life. The sight of her standing so proud and majestic in the centre of Her sanctuary made Ellie's heart swell with pride. She smiled at Yvette as they moved to place their hands against the smooth bark of Her trunk. The Tree responded to their touch immediately.

Aahh, daughter of the Stars. Your presence fills me with pleasure. What brings you to My home this day?

We are here to ask for Your help, Mother Tree. Something is wrong with Jayce...

The Tree quivered under their hands. *So it has begun?*

What? How did you—?

The madness caused by the bond was foreseen by the Stars. I'm sorry Ellie... but the bonding was a necessary part of your journey.

Anger and pain boiled inside Ellie's chest. *You mean you knew? Why didn't you warn us?*

I am not allowed to interfere in these matters. I cannot reveal what is foreseen by the Stars until after a prophecy is invoked.

What prophecy? What the hell are you talking about? We saved your life, and this is how you repay us?

I am truly sorry, your despair pains Me. Ask the questions to which you desire answers, and I will try to answer them.

Something about the way the Tree worded that last statement made Ellie stop and think for a minute. She suspected the Tree could only answer direct questions. She needed to choose her words carefully.

Is there a cure for the madness?

There is.

Can you please tell us what the cure is? Or where we can find it?

I do not know the answer to either of those questions.

Right, so what about the prophecy? Where can I read it?

The prophecy is contained in the Book of Time. The Book's whereabouts is unknown to me.

So the book is hidden somewhere then? If I find the book, I'll be able to read the prophecy?

Correct.

And it will tell me about how the curse works?

I have no knowledge of the Book's contents.

Ellie looked at Yvette in desperation. She couldn't think of how to word any other questions.

Is the Book hidden in this world? Yvette asked softly

No, Mother to the daughter of the Stars. The Book is not in this world.

So, you don't know where it is, but you know where it's not? Ellie said, frustration making her want to shake the Tree.

The Tree sighed again, as if She wanted to tell them something, but couldn't, unless they asked the right questions. *I'm sorry.*

Damnit. She needed to think. What *were* the right questions? Wait. The Tree said their bond had been necessary... *had been...* Did that mean it might not be 'necessary' any longer?

Will the madness stop if our bond is broken?

Sadness emanated from the Tree before She answered. *Yes*

Yvette sucked in a breath and frowned at Ellie. "But—"

Ellie raised her hand to cut her mother off. *And the bond between witch and familiar is broken only by one or both dying?*

Such is the legendary curse of witch and familiar.

Ellie chewed on her lip. Why hadn't the Tree said 'that is correct' or 'yes'. Maybe not all legends were true or based on hard and fast rules. Sometimes deviations were possible... weren't they?

Are these legends derived from the Book of Time?

The Tree shivered. Was it from excitement? Was Ellie getting close to asking the right questions?

All legends are derived from the Book of Time.

So The Book may hold the answers we're looking for... there is hope?

There is always hope, daughter of the Stars.

So the prophecy could be wrong?

This prophecy... yes.

So there's more than one prophecy?

Many false prophecies exist. The paths chosen determines the outcome of each.

Ellie stared at the Tree in awe. Not all prophecies came true! So, this Book might contain information about another way to break their bond. Something that didn't involve one of them dying.

Thank you, Mother Tree. I'm sure Your help will prove invaluable.

You are very welcome. Two things I must tell you before you leave. First, the Stars would hide the Book of Time where only those in great need will find it. Second, the Stars favour both you and your familiar, as well as your union, so you will achieve more together than apart. You must continue to trust each other, no matter what happens. I wish you luck on your journey.

Ellie and Yvette said a final thank you and farewell, stepped away from the Tree and joined hands. Within seconds, Yvette teleported them back to the hotel in Sydney.

Ellie raced toward Jayce's sleeping figure. She lifted his head from the floor and slid herself underneath, so he rested in her lap. She ran her hands through his thick unruly hair, her eyes filling with tears. *Everything's gonna be okay babe. I know what we need to do now. Nothing and no one is going to take you away from me. I promise.*

Ellie became aware of the heavy silence hanging in the air. Jasper, Isabel and Iridia hadn't said a word, but their faces were etched with worry lines. She turned to Yvette. "Can you tell them what happened please? I just need some time..."

Yvette sighed and nodded. She moved over to sit with their friends and began to repeat what the Tree told them. Ellie zoned out, needing to process what she'd learned. Jayce's handsome face was peaceful, the pain at bay for the time being. But how long would that last after they woke him up?

Ellie gritted her teeth and smoothed the hair back from Jayce's forehead. Whatever happened, she wouldn't let the madness take him. If she had to die to save him, then so be it. They would search for The Book of Time together, and she would trust that their love was strong enough to stave off the curse until they found it.

CHAPTER SIXTEEN

Jayce

*J*ayce slept... his mind adrift in a sea of madness. Anger rippled along every nerve ending. He needed to find an outlet. Hate filled his every thought. He craved magic... and he knew exactly where to find it. His witch had all the magic he would ever need.

An image of Ellie's smiling face flashed into his head. Guilt and shame consumed him. How could he even *think* about hurting her? The woman he loved more than life itself. He squashed the poisonous thoughts down, filling his mind with images of his beautiful morwitch.

He recalled his excitement when he first found Ellie in the Dragon realm. But then he'd discovered she didn't remember him. The sense of loss and betrayal had almost crippled him. How had she forgotten what they meant to each other? No, none of this was her fault. Thomas was the monster responsible for all his pain. Jayce's rage flared anew. He wanted to rip the man apart with his bare hands.

As the hate surged to the surface again, so did the craving for the magic. Writhing beneath his skin like an insatiable hunger eating away at his soul. But taking Ellie's magic would hurt her. Damnit. There had to be another way. But then, why should *she* hold all the power. He was the man! It should be his to control. He was sick of picking up her scraps and riding on her apron strings. The power should belong to him!

But he loved her! A memory of her frightened face and her words slipped into his befuddled mind. She said she would happily give him all her magic. He sighed as the rage subsided again. Ellie loved him unconditionally. What the hell was wrong with him?

And so the conflict continued. Every time he clawed his way toward the sane and lucid thoughts, they were devoured by the hate and anger of his madness. Relief washed over him as he finally woke from the nightmare.

"Wow... I just had the worst nightmare—" The words froze in his throat at the wariness and fear on the faces of his friends and family. How had he ended up on the floor with his head in Ellie's lap? He'd felt her caressing his forehead when he woke, but she pulled her hands away as soon as he spoke. The flash of fear in her eyes made him want to shrivel up and die. "Okay, so I'm guessing it wasn't a nightmare? What happened?"

Yvette cleared her throat. "I'm sorry Jayce, but I put

you to sleep. You lost control while using Ellie's magic. I was worried you might... hurt her."

Jayce sat up and pulled Ellie into his arms. "Oh sweetheart, I am *so* sorry. Please tell me you believe I'd never hurt you?"

Ellie had stiffened when he first reached for her, but only for a heartbeat. Then she relaxed against him and sighed. "Of course I believe you. I trust you to always keep me safe."

Yvette cleared her throat... again. "Jayce, we've been busy while you were asleep. Ellie and I paid a quick visit to the Tree of Life, which proved very enlightening." Yvette proceeded to tell him everything the Tree said. By the time she was finished, he wanted to throw up.

Stars... what if this madness could actually make him hurt Ellie? No, that must never be allowed to happen. Someone needed to stop him long before he could become a threat. "Jasper... if I—"

"Don't say it son... I'm sure it won't come to that." Jayce locked eyes with the old dragon, begging him to acknowledge what he was asking, until Jasper finally sighed and nodded. His old friend would do what was necessary to protect Ellie if and when the time came.

"Won't come to what? Jayce, what are you talking about?"

"It's nothing babe, let it go. So... do we all agree then? The Book of Time is hidden somewhere on Brevis?"

Yvette nodded. "Yes, I agree Jayce. But I don't think you'll find the same Brevis you went to last time. From what I can gather, Brevis assumes whatever world the visitor *needs*. So this time you won't be looking for The Living Lake, and if the Stars were determined to keep the Book of Time hidden, who knows what it'll be like."

Jayce ran his shaking hands through his hair. "Okay, so how are we gonna do this? The Tree made it abundantly clear we need to find the Book together, but I can't guarantee I can hold off the... madness... until we find it."

He ground the last words out through clenched teeth, horrified by the thought of harming Ellie. Anger and hate simmered just below the surface, and he was powerless to stop its progression. But he would kill himself before he allowed his traitorous mind and body to hurt the woman he loved.

Ellie

ELLIE'S HEART ached at the agony on Jayce's face. But instead of running away, her arms tightened protectively around him. "We'll beat this Jayce. I won't let the madness take you... I promise. But we can only do this together. I love you... and I refuse to even contemplate the thought of living without you." She turned to Yvette. "There must be something we can do to delay its progress. What about the spell to slow time we used on the Tree of Life?"

Yvette shook her head. "No, everything in his body would slow down. He wouldn't be able to function at all."

"What about something like the memory wiping spell? It seems to work by blocking off access to the part of the brain containing memories. What if we tried to block off the section dealing with emotions? Sort of like a pain block, but for emotions instead."

"Ellie you're a genius. That might work. But you do realise the spell will block *all* emotion?" Yvette turned to Jayce. "You would be living in an emotionless void. And there's a possibility you may lose some of the memories associated with those emotions."

Jayce shrugged. "I'm prepared to try anything that'll guarantee Ellie's safety. If you think this will work, let's give it a go."

"Hey, don't I have any say in this?" Ellie said, throwing her hands in the air. "Because if my fiancé is going to be in an emotionless vacuum for the next however long, we *will* be having some alone time first!"

Ellie's face burned as they all stared at her in shock. What the hell? This wasn't about them. If Jayce was going to be incapable of feeling anything, she had every right to demand some time alone while his emotions were still intact.

Jayce chuckled. "Try arguing with *that* logic. I must admit, when Ellie didn't recognise me for those few days, I nearly went insane. I understand you're all worried I'll hurt her, but I'm sure I can control myself for another hour at least."

Isabel stood and went into bat for them. "You heard

the girl, she needs some time alone with her man." She smiled at Ellie and Jayce. "One hour guys, and we'll be back."

Isabel waved aside Jasper and Yvette's protests and ushered them out of the room. She winked as she pulled the door shut behind them.

Ellie giggled at the relief on Jayce's face. "By the way, be grateful I didn't tell them I know *exactly* what stops you from having the bad thoughts."

Jayce pulled her into his lap and laid his forehead against hers. "I wouldn't have cared what you told them if this was the end result. It feels like I only just got you back and now I'm losing you again. Remember how we promised ourselves a week where we locked the rest of the world out? I'm starting to think that's never going to happen."

"Well, at least we'll be doing this together. Even if I won't have *all* of you, it's still better than being apart."

"Damnit Elle, why does this crap keep happening? Why can't the world just leave us alone?"

"I'm hoping this Book of Time will give us the answers to all those questions. If we *are* part of some prophecy, I want to find out what it is and be done with it. *Then* we might be allowed to have a life. I told you... I'll do whatever's necessary to break this curse!"

"I love you... don't ever question that. My brain may forget for a while, but my heart won't. Nothing will ever stop me from loving you... okay?"

Ellie nodded, her eyes filling with tears. Without Jayce in her life, she would never be whole again. But *her* Jayce would disappear while-ever the spell was in place, and what remained would be an emotionless shell. She needed to store the memories of his loving smile, his eyes when they smouldered with passion and his ever-protective warm embrace.

Her fears were mirrored in Jayce's eyes as he read her thoughts. They didn't even know how long the spell would need to be in place, or what the after-effects would be. What if he didn't still feel the same after...? No, there must be another way. But before she was able to voice her objections, Jayce's lips sealed off her words.

The kiss was bitter-sweet. Jayce's out of control emotions tumbled over themselves, trying to convince her everything would be okay. She melted against him, pushing aside the fear and doubts and focusing on the here and now. She cupped his face with her hands, memorising the sensation of being surrounded by his love. No matter what happened, she would savour the next hour, basking in the warmth of his love.

CHAPTER SEVENTEEN

Ellie

*E*llie watched as the spell took effect, the animation in Jayce's face replaced by a blank stare. "Right. So, what did I miss? Why is everyone looking at me?" he said in a detached, disinterested voice.

Ellie was torn between relief that the spell had worked and a depressing sense of isolation. Her Jayce was completely gone. Stars, what if their bond didn't work with Jayce's emotions shut down? Focusing on Jayce's expressionless eyes, she sent him a message.

Jayce... can you still hear me?

Yes Ellie. Why would you think I'd not be able to?

Ellie groaned at the robotic tone in his voice. If they didn't find this damn Book soon, *she* might be the one to go mad.

Jayce scanned the room and blinked. That was about

the only way to describe his lack of facial expression. "When do we leave for Brevis?"

Yvette eyed Ellie warily before answering. "Do you remember why you need to go to Brevis, Jayce?"

Jayce stared at her. "Of course I remember. To find the Book of Time. My brain is still perfectly intact. Now can you all please stop gawking at me like I'm some kind of lab-rat. I'm fine!"

Yvette shook her head at his abrupt tone, her eyes full of sympathy as she turned to Ellie. "Right. So, you'll both need new glamours, and then we'll do the same as when you travelled to Brevis before. I'll teleport Jayce to the Dragon Realm and come back for Ellie. You'll have to travel separately again, but at least this time the Aqueous flow won't be tainted."

Ellie shuddered at the memories Yvette's words evoked. The last time they travelled in the flow, their memories had been twisted, until each believed the other had betrayed them. Without thinking, she reached for Jayce's hand as the painful memories surfaced, needing his energy and reassurance.

Jayce frowned as Ellie's hand reached for his. "Not now Ellie. We need to get moving."

Ellie gasped, stuffing her hand into her pocket. She had to keep reminding herself he wasn't *her* Jayce. And if she ever wanted *him* back, they needed to speed things up a bit.

"Wait. Since I know exactly where the entrance to the pool is, couldn't I teleport straight there and dive in this time? It's not like we have to worry about anyone following my magic trail. And I wouldn't even need a glamour."

Yvette frowned and chewed her lip. "I suppose you're right. I just hate the thought of you going alone."

Ellie smiled and shook her head. She waited for the usual protest from Jayce, but he seemed totally uninterested in the subject. Of course. Worry over her safety would be the last thing *this* Jayce would ever consider.

"I'll be fine mother. What if Jayce drew a map to the pool inside the Dragon Council chambers? Then you could take him directly there too?"

"Yes, I can do that. And I agree with Ellie, it would be much more logical and less time consuming.

Ellie groaned and turned away. Maybe she should ask Yvette to put a glamour on him, one she couldn't see through, so he didn't look like Jayce at all. At least that might stop her wanting to punch him in the face every time he opened his mouth.

She took a deep breath and gave herself a mental slap. *None of this was Jayce's fault!* He simply wasn't capable of functioning at any other level. This wasn't about how *she* felt. She'd keep her mind focused on their goal. Jayce's sanity. Even if she was in serious danger of losing her own along the way.

Jayce

JAYCE SCRATCHED HIS HEAD, unable to understand Ellie's ridiculous expectations. He had no desire for physical contact whatsoever and couldn't fathom why she wanted him to hold her hand. They had a job to do, and her behaviour was nothing short of irrational. It might be simpler if he avoided eye contact as well. Because every time he spoke, she looked like she wanted to stab him.

The whole situation was weird enough, without having to deal with her emotional problems. This 'mission' was all he could focus on. In fact, nothing else in his life seemed to exist. He studied the people sitting in the room, Jasper, Isabel and his mother, and felt nothing. Oh well... not his problem. He would do what he deemed necessary to survive, and no more.

Jayce walked over to the writing desk in the corner of the room and began drawing the map Yvette would need to teleport them to the opening of the Aqueous flow, inside the Dragon Council meeting room. No one spoke, and he got the impression they were all still staring at him.

"Perhaps you should come and watch me do this Yvette, so I can explain as I go," he said without looking up.

Seriously, what was wrong with these people? They were supposed to be here to do a job. And the sooner the better. He couldn't wait to remove himself from their constant 'vigilance'.

Yvette moved over to stand next to him, and he

launched into a detailed description of the castle layout. Satisfied she had a clear picture in her head, he looked at Ellie.

"So are we ready to go?" Her eyes were filled with hurt, and he tried to think of something to say. But he just didn't seem to have any appropriate words. He shrugged and returned his attention to Yvette and the map.

"What if something goes wrong?" Ellie said through gritted teeth. He looked up to find the hurt replaced by a frosty indifference. Good. She would probably be easier to deal with in this frame of mind anyway. "I mean, no one should be expecting us to go to Brevis, but what if the Councils decided to post a guard at the entrance pools? What if... one of us... doesn't make it?"

"Then finding the Book of Time will no longer be necessary. If one of us is dead, the other will be free." From the shock on the faces of everyone in the room he assumed his words had sounded callous. He ran his hand through his hair... he'd only been stating the facts.

"I'm afraid Jayce is right honey." Well at least Yvette appeared to be able to grasp the obvious. "If either of you doesn't show up, the other is to come back straight away. There's no point in looking for the Book if—"

"Don't worry mother... I get it." She turned toward Jayce and shrugged. "Well, I guess this is it. I'll see you on Brevis... good luck," she said, and left without another word.

Yvette placed her hand on Jayce's shoulder. "Just find the Book and come back as soon as you can. I know you don't remember or feel the same way, but Ellie loves you and will do anything to save you. She will take risks she otherwise wouldn't, and you need to protect her with your life. Do you understand what I'm saying?"

Jayce nodded, a nagging emptiness in the region of his heart. He had two jobs... find the Book and guard Ellie with his life. Sounded simple enough...

CHAPTER EIGHTEEN

Ellie

*E*llie smiled with relief. The waters of the entry pool to the Aqueous flow were a startling azure blue and crystal clear. The last time she stood in this place preparing to dive in, the water was a murky brown, compliments of the taint Thomas planted in the flow.

She went over her prepared answers to the Aqueous' usual questions. Taking a deep breath, she dived into the water. She floated for a while, unsure how much time passed before the voice of the Aqueous entered her head. About time! Her lungs were starting to burn from lack of oxygen.

Breathe, the voice said, and Ellie fought the urge to argue.

She knew how the flow worked. The water would turn

to air as soon as she breathed in. Still, the logical part of her brain wanted her to believe she would drown. Pushing the thought to the back of her mind, she opened her mouth and sucked the air into her lungs. She smiled, resisting the temptation to tell that logical part 'I-told-you-so'.

We meet again, Daughter of the Stars. What do you require from Brevis this time?

I need to find the Book of Time.

The voice fell silent for a moment. *The Book has been hidden for centuries. What makes you think you will find it on Brevis?*

Because there is nowhere else it can be. I have a need, which Brevis must fulfil.

The voice chuckled. *You have grown much since our last meeting. Whatever will be will be.*

Ellie waited for the voice to continue, but silence surrounded her once again. She relaxed and went back to floating in the void, keeping her mind focused on their search for the Book of Time and saving *her* Jayce. She shied away from scrolling through happy memories of their time together, not wanting to repeat the experience of the last time she used the flow.

Nothing mattered but finding the Book. Thoughts she'd kept hidden when she thought Jayce close enough to read her mind rose to the surface. She would not let Jayce either die or go mad. She already blamed herself for stealing his future away because of the bond. The man had suffered enough because of their accidental crossing of paths.

If one of them must die to break the curse, it would be her. A future without Jayce was inconceivable.

The sensation of floating vanished, and she felt herself falling. Brevis awaited her below. Taking a deep breath, she smiled. *Whatever will be will be...*

Jayce

JAYCE STARED into the waters of the entrance to the Aqueous flow. The pool appeared different to the last time... cleaner perhaps?

Thanking Yvette for her assistance, he dived into the pool. He had a job to do, and he needed to get on with it. He floated in the water, waiting for the voice.

Breathe, the voice in his head said. Without hesitation, he opened his mouth and sucked in the air. He understood the instructions.

Welcome back Son of the Stars. Why do you wish to travel to Brevis this time?

I must find the Book of Time.

Silence. Then one word entered his head. *Why?*

Because I've been tasked with the job of finding it.

Why? The voice repeated.

Jayce searched his mind for an answer that would satisfy the voice. Why *did* they need the Book? It had something to do with a problem caused by the bond between him and Ellie, but he hadn't really questioned *why* they needed it. Maybe this had something to do with emotions? That would explain why Ellie kept looking so disappointed.

I don't know why. But apparently, there is a need, and I believe the Book is somewhere on Brevis. Jayce waited for the voice's response. His answer sounded lame, but he couldn't think of anything else to say.

You have spoken the truth. For that I will grant you passage. I fear you are broken and need answers. Only Time will tell.

What do you mean I'm broken? No reply. He shook his head, dismissing what the voice said as irrational. Surely, he would know if he was broken?

Jayce floated mindlessly in the void. By the time he arrived on Brevis, Ellie should be waiting for him. Every time he thought about her, a knot formed in his stomach, as if he should *feel* something when he was around her. Yvette said she loved him. But he had no concept of the feelings associated with that word. He had no idea what her expectations concerning him were.

He realised he was falling just before he hit the ground. Pushing all thoughts of Ellie aside, he prepared himself to do his job. He would find the Book of Time and protect Ellie... then he could finally be left alone.

Ellie

ELLIE'S HEART sunk as she took in the barren landscape. Nothing but cracked, dry earth, the plant-life sparse and stunted. This was a very different Brevis to the one that held The Living Lake. The eerie stillness in the air made her shiver, sweat rolling down her back. This place gave her the creeps.

A scream pierced the silence. She spun to find a dark, twisted looking wyvern flying towards her. Panic numbed her mind and scrambled her thoughts. How did they bring the wyverns down last time? Damnit... she couldn't remember!

The memory broke through the numbness fogging her brain. The sleeping spell. Lifting her arm, she directed the spell at the rapidly approaching creature. But the wyvern's wings didn't miss a beat, eyes boring into her as it homed in on its prey. The spell didn't work. What if her magic didn't...? Of course! Jayce had been there to help her. She needed his strength behind her magic.

An almighty roar sounded from behind her, and then Jayce's gleaming copper dragon body flew over her head as her legs turned to jelly and folded beneath her. Jayce ducked and weaved, skilfully avoiding the wyvern's poisonous barbed tail as he released a stream of fire. The creature saw Jayce too late to retreat from the much larger dragon. Within seconds, it was consumed in flames, screaming as it plummeted to its death. Ellie watched in awe as Jayce hovered over the dying wyvern, then banked and headed back to where she sat.

He morphed back into his human form as soon as his feet hit the ground, and Ellie jumped up and threw herself at him. He stiffened as she wrapped her arms around his waist, but she didn't care whether he returned the embrace or not. For now, she was content with the warmth of his body against hers, his strength restoring her equilibrium.

"Ummm... are you okay? Did the beast hurt you?"

Ellie tipped her head back, surprised by the question. He almost sounded like he cared. His eyes were filled with confusion, his arms remaining stiffly by his side, and his entire body rigid.

Ellie sighed and stepped backwards. "I'm fine. Sorry about that, I keep forgetting you're not..."

"I'm not what?" Jayce tilted his head to the side.

"Forget I said anything. You wouldn't understand," she said, brushing the dirt off her jeans and pulling herself together. How could she explain she wanted him to hold her in his arms and whisper that everything would be alright? The Jayce standing in front of her would never get that in a million years.

Jayce

JAYCE WAS CONFUSED by the disappointment in her eyes. He scratched his head, wondering what he did wrong this time. He'd seen the wyvern diving toward her when he landed on Brevis, and his dragon attacked and killed the creature. What more did she want from him? Yvette said to protect her, and that's exactly what he did.

He shook his head and viewed the harsh landscape surrounding them. Why didn't they think to bring food or water with them? They wouldn't survive long in this climate without some form of sustenance.

"Does your magic work here?"

"I'm not sure. I tried to use a sleep spell on the wyvern like we did before, but it had no effect. I don't know whether it was because my magic doesn't work, or I wasn't strong enough alone."

Jayce nodded and continued to scour the area for any signs of life. "Okay, so how about you try to fetch a couple of bottles of water from the fridge in our hotel room. Because if you can't, we may be in trouble."

Ellie sighed and held out both hands in front of her. A bottle appeared in each hand, and he nodded in satisfaction.

"Excellent. Now, I suggest we explore this place from the sky. We could be wandering around for days on foot, and I'd like to get this over with."

Without another word, he morphed into his dragon form and swung his tail for her to climb on. Ellie muttered and cursed in her head as she settled on his back, and he decided to ignore her. What was the point of

continuing a conversation that made absolutely no sense
whatsoever?

CHAPTER NINETEEN

Ellie

*E*llie clenched her knees firmly against Jayce's scaly neck as he launched into the sky. He'd been right about one thing... they needed this to be over. Scanning the barren wastelands below them, she sighed in frustration. How the hell would they find a Book in the middle of nowhere?

A shiver ran down her spine at the sensation of being watched. She scanned the skies in panic, but not another single living creature was in sight. So where had the wyvern come from? Its friends must be around here somewhere. Maybe they'd seen what happened and were waiting to make their move.

Yes, there's bound to be others hiding close-by. I'll try to navigate towards the centre of the world. From memory, that's about where we found The Living Lake. It could be a pattern used in all the worlds.

Sounds like a plan. Keep your eye out for some type of structure. The Book would need to be protected from the elements. Wait. What's that? In front of us and slightly to the left. Why would four trees be grouped together like? From what I've seen so far, trees are about as rare as hen's teeth here. See how they form a canopy where they meet? I reckon they've been planted to hide something from view.

Hmmm... I suppose it's possible. Might be worth taking a look. His lack of enthusiasm made her want to scream, but she bit back her angry retort. What was the point? He wasn't capable of expressing himself any other way.

Jayce landed near the circle of trees, and she scrambled towards his tail. Her heart raced with excitement. A structure stood in the middle of the trees.

Don't even think *about entering those trees without me! We have no idea what kind of danger could be lurking in there. Something tells me the Book will be well guarded. Remember the trial we had to go through to retrieve the water from The Living Lake?*

Ellie waited patiently for Jayce to morph back into his human form and then launched. "Listen here you! I realise you have no memory of us ever being close, but don't you dare ever speak to me in that tone of voice again. I am not a five-year-old and you will not order me around. Are we clear?"

Jayce stared at her and blinked. Seriously? That was all he had? She *so* wanted to slap the blank indifference off his face and shake him until he remembered everything.

Damnit, this was all too hard! She hadn't realised until now how much she relied on Jayce's constant love, support and encouragement. She didn't want to be brave and 'save the world' without him. Instead, she wanted to go home and crawl into bed.

She sunk to the ground as the tears started to fall. Looking at Jayce and not being able to touch him was like a form of torture. She'd never felt so alone. Even when she escaped from Thomas, Jayce's voice had been in her head, encouraging her and making her feel loved. Life was so unfair. Why couldn't the world leave them alone and let them be together?

Wiping the tears away, she looked up to find Jayce's eyes on her. "Sorry about that. Just needed a quick meltdown for a minute. I'll be fine in a second."

"I'm sorry too," he said, confusion in his eyes. "I know I'm not who you want me to be at the moment, but I don't know how to be any different. How about we at least try to be friends? I'll try not to speak so abruptly, if you can try not to expect more than I'm capable of giving. Deal?" He held out his hand and helped her to her feet, quick to step back as she stood.

"Deal. And I'll also try and refrain from being such a snarky cow." Did she imagine it, or did his lip twitch?

"Okay, so let's go check out what the trees are hiding, shall we?"

The structure was made of stone and stood almost as tall as the trees surrounding it. Ellie shivered. It reminded her of a burial crypt—one of those huge things rich people bury all their family members in. They walked around the perimeter of the imposing structure but couldn't see an opening.

Ellie frowned. "So what do we do now? This has got to be where the Book is hidden, but how do we get inside?"

Jayce shook his head. "Your guess is as good as mine."

Ellie sighed and moved closer to the seamless stone wall, rubbing her hands across the smooth surface. "Well, the only thing we know for sure about Brevis, is that whatever it holds only appears when there's a *need*. So obviously we *need* the Book, and we *need* to find a way in. Can't get much *needier* than that!"

She jumped back in surprise as the wall started to vibrate under her hand. A groaning sound emanated from somewhere inside the structure. Ellie's mouth dropped open as the section of wall under her hands shuddered and began to sink slowly into the ground in front of her. Jayce moved to stand beside her, neither of them speaking as the wall slid downwards and disappeared.

"Woah... did that door really open because I said I *needed* it to?"

"Well, it sure looked that way. Hey, do you think you could fetch us a couple of torches? I'd rather not be stumbling around in the dark."

Yeah sure... she'd just pull one out of thin air! Where the hell would she find...? The aunts. They always kept torches in the storeroom at her home back in Darwin. Ellie held out her hands, closed her eyes and pictured the shelf where she'd last seen them. Instantly a torch appeared in each hand. She smiled, checked they both worked and handed one to Jayce.

Jayce raised an eyebrow, and she shrugged. "The aunts always keep a few torches handy in case of black-outs.

And we'd better return them when we're finished. They'll throw a fit if they're not where they left them."

Jayce nodded and shone the torch into the entrance. Ellie shuddered at the sight of the stone stairs descending into darkness. "Of course we need to go underground. Why would I think the damned Book would be sitting on a table just inside the door?"

Jayce reached for her hand and Ellie's eyes flew to his face in surprise. He shrugged. "It's dark and the stairs are pretty steep. I don't want us getting separated. Are you ready?"

"Ready as I'll ever be," Ellie said as she placed her hand in his. His energy seeped into her the minute his hand closed around hers, and from the way Jayce's hand twitched, he felt it too. Her heart ached at the confusion in his eyes. He opened his mouth to say something and then shook his head. "Let's go," he mumbled, and they stepped through the doorway hand in hand.

CHAPTER TWENTY

Jayce

Keeping a tight grip on Ellie's hand, Jayce descended into the darkness, the beam of the torch hardly penetrating the inky silence. The sensations raging through his body since taking her hand made his head spin. Almost as if he *should* feel something. Apparently, even though his *brain* held no memory of ever experiencing strong emotions, his body seemed more than willing to compensate.

Her touch elicited sensations he couldn't even describe. *Wait... were these feelings emotions?* No wonder everyone made such a fuss about them. But whatever the cause, his body wanted to prolong the connection, even if his mind couldn't process what was happening. In fact, his body seemed to have detached itself from his brain, intent on following its own path.

The cold, stale air carried the smell of death and decay.

How long since another living creature had entered what was beginning to feel like a tomb? The area around them expanded, until they walked on a stairway that appeared to be suspended in mid-air. He shuddered, wondering if the hard part wasn't so much getting *inside* this place, but rather getting *out*.

You okay back there? He messaged Ellie, feeling her hand shaking in his.

Y-yep. Just keep going... I need this to be over. Interesting train of thought going through your head by the way. You're doing an excellent job of keeping both our minds distracted.

Her silent laughter chuckling softly in his mind made his stomach churn. What was *that* all about? He shrugged, enjoying the unfamiliar sensations washing over him way too much to stop now.

Ellie gasped and pulled him back. *Jayce, you're not supposed to be thinking like that. It's dangerous for you to feel any kind of emotion.*

But I thought you wanted me to... Damn woman, you are the strangest, most confusing person I have ever met. But right now, we need to get to the bottom of this staircase and find the Book. Everything else can wait until we're out of here.

No argument from me on that point. Can you see the end yet?

Nope, it's like there's nothing there. In any direction.

Fighting the distraction of the unfamiliar thoughts running riot inside his head, he shone the beam of his torch around them. Intent on locating the 'missing' walls and ceiling, he stepped down and gasped as the stone began to crumble beneath his foot. He staggered, trying to shift his weight back to the step behind him. Too late. His body continued forward onto the rapidly disintegrating step.

Ellie tried to reach for him with her free hand. Terrified of taking her with him, he pushed her away releasing the hand he'd been holding. *Ellie... turn around and go back... NOW!* His mind yelled as he toppled sideways into the abyss. *I love you...*

Ellie

"Jaaaaayce... Noooooo..." Ellie screamed, as his body disappeared into the darkness. She slumped down on the step as her legs turned to jelly, too stunned to move. This couldn't be happening. They came here to *save* Jayce. It couldn't have all been for nothing! For an instant, she considered giving up and following him...

Stop being ridiculous Ellie and pull yourself together. If Jayce had somehow survived, he needed her help. Pushing down the sobs threatening to explode from her throat, she concentrated on slowing her breathing.

Okay, so now what? No way in hades she was turning around and going back without Jayce. She had to find him. He could be hurt and unconscious. How would she even know whether he was still alive?

Wait... maybe he didn't fall that far. They'd been walking downhill for a while. What if they were almost at the bottom of the staircase?

"Jayce... can you hear me?" Her voice echoed in the vast space, her heart pounding so loud she worried she wouldn't hear his answer. She held her breath... nothing.

Panic surged again. *No, that doesn't mean he's dead! He could just be unconscious.* But how would she know...? A memory surfaced. Jayce had told her something about their bond creating a kind of 'heart echo'. That's how he knew she was still alive when Thomas took her. Well, if he could find it, then so could she.

Closing her eyes, she took a couple of deep shuddering breaths, concentrating on her own heartbeat. Damn. It was beating way too fast... how the hell was she supposed to hear an echo? She needed to calm down. Easier said than done. The sensation of being suspended in mid-air, in a huge black underground hole, all alone, was *not* helping.

Okay, focus on some pleasant memories. Yeah, 'cos there'd been *so* many of those lately. She shrugged, scrolling through her memories, lingering on those where she and Jayce were relaxed and happy. *Damn, they were few and far between.* But it seemed to be working. Her heart-rate had almost returned to normal. So now... and there it was. A soft weak echo. Jayce was alive!

Thank the Stars. Relief flooded through her tired body. Right, so he was alive, and he needed her. So how the hell did she find him? Teleporting was out; that required a clear image of the place she wanted to go.

Unless? What if she tried to use Jayce himself as the focal point? Yvette had never mentioned whether it was possible or not. But hey, nothing she and Jayce did half the time should be possible.

She sent a silent prayer to the Stars. Not that she expected them to care. But she had no-one else to ask. If this didn't work, she had no idea where she would end up, but it was worth the risk. Jayce needed her... subject closed.

Ellie closed her eyes, took a deep, shaky breath, and focused on the image of Jayce in her mind. Instantly, the stone step under her feet slipped away to be replaced by dirt. Opening her eyes, she found Jayce's still form sprawled on the ground. The spell worked! She dropped down beside him, her chest aching as the long-suppressed sobs escaped. Damn she loved that face!

Jayce stirred at her touch and opened his eyes. "I thought I told you to turn around and go back? How the hell did you find me?"

"Ssshh... don't talk. I teleported to you. Instead of a place, I pictured you, wherever you were. Now I need to heal you. Where does it hurt?"

"Ummm... everywhere?" he said with a grimace.

"Okay babe... I'll see what I can do." She brushed the hair back from his pain-filled face, her hands shaking as she tried to assess the damage. "Just hold on..."

Ellie hesitated, unsure where to focus her magic. Most of the injuries would more than likely be internal. So she directed her first spell toward his organs, relieved as some of the pain faded from his face.

"Do you think any bones are broken?"

"Well I can't feel anything from the waist down, and I landed on my back, so...?"

Ellie's breath hitched at the thought of him suffering from spinal damage. What if his injuries were beyond her power to heal? She pushed the thought aside, casting more spells, until she was hit by a wave of exhaustion. She needed to eat, drink and sleep to restore her magic.

A grin spread across Jayce's face. "Damn it's good to be able to move. Thank you, sweetheart. You're amazing... you know that right?"

Ellie tried to return the smile, her mind and body aching with fatigue. She laid her head down on Jayce's chest as he gathered her into his embrace. Being back in his arms made everything better. She couldn't remember the last time...

She lifted her head and looked into Jayce's eyes, her conflicting emotions battling in her head. "Jayce, you're *you* again. I can't decide whether to be over-the-moon or worried sick."

"And you are exhausted." He eased her head back down against his chest. "Sshh... don't start freaking out on me babe. The anger hasn't resurfaced yet, so hopefully the spell has some kind of residual effect. But whatever happens, you need to eat, drink and sleep. Any chance you can fetch something?"

Ellie sighed, content to lie here forever, his steady heartbeat comforting beneath her head. She pointed to the ground beside them and a bottle of water, and some pre-packaged sandwiches appeared. "I remembered seeing them in the hotel fridge. Thought they might be better than junk food."

Jayce leaned down and kissed the top of her head. "That's my girl."

Ellie smiled. She didn't care what trials they still had to go through, at least they would be together. She had *her* Jayce back, and everything else paled to insignificance. Jayce shifted and reached for the packaged sandwiches. He nudged her gently and she lifted her head to look at him.

"Here sweetheart," he said, holding out half a sandwich. "Before you go to sleep."

She smiled and took the sandwich from him. The food tasted like cardboard, but her body needed the sustenance, so she ate the whole thing. She took a couple of swigs from the bottle of water, and then settled back against Jayce's chest.

She wanted to stay awake and soak up the sensations flooding through her at having her Jayce back, but her body's need for sleep overpowered her. She drifted off wrapped in the comfort of his arms.

CHAPTER TWENTY-ONE

Jayce

*J*ayce closed his eyes as a single tear ran down his face, overwhelmed and humbled by his love for this woman in his arms. He'd told her to go, to get out of this tomb they entered so full of hope. And he had expected to die, accepting his fate as the price for Ellie's survival. Then her hand had touched his face, and he'd thought she was an angel come to take him to the afterlife.

When he finally opened his eyes to find his brave, stubborn, beautiful morwitch sitting beside him, his heart melted. He knew his body was broken, that he was dying. But the Stars granted him one more wish—the chance to say goodbye. He wouldn't die sad and alone, Ellie was here with him.

And then Ellie performed her miracle. She healed him. Just like that, his pain was gone and his body repaired.

She risked everything to bring him back from the brink of death.

He smiled as he remembered the moment the spell blocking his emotions broke. Refusing to let her help him and put herself at risk, he pushed her away from him as he fell. Something inside him snapped. He couldn't die without telling her how much he loved her. So his brain simply removed the barriers raised by the spell, shouting the words she needed to hear.

So, their love had proven stronger than a spell yet again. Even while under Thomas' memory spell, Ellie's flashbacks of their time together had broken through. Obviously, these spells were designed to control the mind, but sometimes the heart has a mind of its own.

He sighed as Ellie twitched in his arms. His body needed sleep too. And his gut told him their trials were far from over. They both needed to regain their strength before they faced whatever crap the universe threw at them next.

Ellie

ELLIE OPENED her eyes and froze. A gurgling, snuffling sound came from somewhere close-by. She held her breath and waited for her eyes to adjust to the darkness.

Something big slithered across the ground toward them. Every few seconds, it stopped, lifting its head, and sniffing the air.

She pressed her hand against Jayce's chest. *Jayce, wake up. Try not to make any sudden movements. We've got company.*

Jayce stiffened and then gasped. *What the hell is that?*

No idea, but I think there's more than one. Don't move, I don't think they can see us. They keep sniffing the air, like they're drawn to our scent. I'm gonna try a power thrust. But I'll probably need your help. My energy levels could do with a boost.

Ummm, Elle. We've never done this one together. What can I do? You don't use any words when you do this, do you?

Nope, but it usually helps if I'm angry. And right now, I'm good and angry. I am sick to death of things trying to kill us. How about you try to focus your energy on me, and we'll hope for the best.

I love you Elle... my energy is yours to use for as long as you need.

His arms tightened around her, and Ellie's eyes widened in shock as Jayce's energy rushed into her. The possibilities created through their bond never ceased to amaze her. Overflowing with an abundance of energy, she sat up and threw her arm out in the direction of the slithering shadows.

Screams filled the cavern, echoing off the walls around them as dozens of creatures resembling giant worms flew through the air and splattered against the walls, exploding like bugs crushed under a shoe. Ellie covered her mouth and swallowed back the bile rising in her throat. The whole thing was too gross for words.

Jayce sat up beside her, his mouth hanging open. "Okay... I guess that worked."

"Wow! Jayce, you're incredible. Your energy literally flooded into me. A totally different feeling to when we cast spells together. More like you were inside me, and we were one person. And I'm not exhausted either. Hey..." She chewed her lip, staring into Jayce's eyes as her mind processed a new possibility. "I wonder if..."

"What? I recognise that look, and it usually means trouble. What are you thinking?"

"Well... what if there was a way to beat the curse *without* the Book of Time?"

"This I've gotta hear. Come on, enough with the suspense. What's your idea?"

Ellie reached up and held his face between her hands. "I want to try to *give* you some of my magic. Your own, to use however and whenever you want. I don't know if—"

Jayce's lips on hers silenced her explanation. She drank him in, welcoming him back from the emotionless void. She pushed away all thoughts of where they were and the creatures trying to kill them, revelling in the sensation of being suspended in a time and place where nothing or no one could intrude. A whimper escaped as Jayce began to pull them back. He lifted his head, and she sighed, the reality of their situation crashing back in.

"I'm sorry baby, but this isn't exactly the time or the place to—"

Ellie smiled sheepishly. "Yeah, yeah... I know. But a girl can wish, can't she?"

Jayce threw his head back and laughed. She couldn't remember the last time he'd laughed like that. The thought made her all the more determined to try and make her plan work. She wanted him to have his own magic... she wanted *this* man back in her life. The one who laughed and cried and loved unashamedly, not the emotional cripple created by a spell.

"So... enough with the distractions. I seriously think this might work. I'll just do exactly what you did when you gave me your energy. Nothing to lose, right?"

Jayce frowned. "I love you more than words can say for offering to do this. But what if it doesn't work, and the cravings come back when the magic won't transfer?"

Ellie shrugged. "It's a risk I'm willing to take. Call me selfish, but I want more than this half-existence we've being living in. I didn't realise how much I missed your laugh until I heard it again. Jayce, we can beat this. We just need to trust each other."

Jayce nodded, his eyes filling with tears. "I wish I could find the words to tell you how incredible you are. What you're suggesting is a huge risk. What if you lose your magic? What if you give me too much? No Elle, as much as I want to, I can't let you do this."

"Jayce, there are so many 'whatifs' involved I can't even begin to contemplate them. Somehow your body knew how much energy you could afford to give me. To be honest, I don't *care* if you end up with all the magic."

"Way before the madness started, I knew you stressed

about not being powerful enough to protect me. If this works, you'll never have to worry about that again." She blushed at the adoration in his golden eyes. "So there... my secret's out. I'm being selfish again and wanting you to carry the burden of the magic. So, can we *please* stop over-analysing things and at least try?"

Jayce sighed and nodded. "Okay, what do I need to do?"

"Well, I don't think we have to be actually using the magic when I share it. I felt your energy inside me before I even cast the spell. Were you thinking anything else when you sent me the message?"

Jayce shuffled his feet and blushed. "Ummm... only that I didn't care what happened to me. I wanted you to have my energy because you needed it more."

Ellie nodded, her heart swelling with happiness. And he said *she* was special. She took both his hands in hers and gazed into his eyes.

I love you Jayce... my magic is yours to use for as long as you need it.

Jayce shuddered, closing his eyes, and sucking in a deep breath.

Ellie's heart raced. "Jayce? Are you okay? Did it work?"

He opened his eyes, and it was her turn to suck in a breath. His honey-gold eyes glowed, but not in anger. It was completely different. Softer. More like the glow from a warm fireplace, rather than the inferno that erupted when he was angry.

"Well, something happened. I'm sort-of tingling all over."

Ellie punched the air. "Yes! That's how I felt when Yvette woke the magic in me. Come on, I'm dying to see you do something."

Jayce chuckled nervously. "Like what?"

She shook his hands, jumping up and down with excitement. "Who cares? Anything. You've helped me cast heaps of spells. What about you try fetching something? That's an easy one."

Jayce closed his eyes and held his hand out in front of him. He knew what to do. Ellie had taught him when they needed to retrieve clothes from a place she'd never been. Within seconds a bottle of water appeared. He dropped the bottle and picked Ellie up in his arms, spinning around and laughing. "I did it Elle. Did you see that? I used magic!"

He stopped spinning and frowned. "Wait. Now we need to find out whether your magic still works."

Ellie smiled and kissed the frown marring his happiness. She didn't care one way or the other. Knowing they had beaten the curse, and seeing Jayce so happy, meant more to her than having the use of magic any day.

"Please just try something babe... for me?" She couldn't resist his pleading tone, and she nodded.

Ellie was almost certain she still had magic. There was no empty, aching hole in the pit of her stomach like when her magic was bound. Nope, she was fine. So she held out her hand, grinning when a bar of chocolate appeared in her palm. "Mmmm... chocolate. Wanna share?"

Jayce laughed and pulled her against him.

"Is that a no? Awesome. More for me."

Jayce

*J*ayce chewed on the last piece of chocolate, savouring the sugary sweetness and the energy he so badly needed. He shone the beam of his torch around the enormous cavern. Which way led to either the Book of Time or a way out? Wait... was he hallucinating, or was that a faint light glowing in the distance? He nudged Ellie reclining against him.

"So... do you reckon that's a light?

Ellie immediately sat up. "Isn't that where the giant wormy things came from?"

"Yep, sure is. But we can't go back the way we came. I don't know if you noticed, but the stairs have totally disappeared."

Ellie shone her torch above and around them and groaned. "Seriously? How does a staircase made of stone just...? Never mind, forget I asked. So how do we get out of here? It's not like we need the Book anymore. I was kind-of hoping for a quick exit."

"Well, I vote we head toward the light." He scrambled to his feet and held out a hand to Ellie. "Much as I hate to interrupt our pleasant interlude and leave our luxurious surrounds, I'm ready to go back to civilisation."

Ellie spluttered as he pulled her to her feet, using her other hand to slap his arm.

"Ouch... what was that for?" Jayce tried not to smile as he rubbed his arm.

"Pleasant interlude? Apart from this place being where you first got your own magic, and the chocolate, a 'pleasant interlude' is the last thing I'd call *this*."

Jayce laughed and hooked her arm through his. "Fine. So you won't miss this paradise then?

Ellie groaned and nudged him with her hip. "Will you please shut up and move. I am seriously over this place. Not to mention being eager to find that 'certain time and place' you mentioned." He cracked up laughing again. *Cheeky minx.*

How long since they last bantered and teased each other like this? He wanted those times again. Would they ever be able to have a normal life, like their short but blissful respite at Jasper and Isabel's cottage before the world went mad? If not, it definitely wouldn't be from lack of trying.

The light emanated from another cavern not far in front of them. Ellie pulled him to a stop before they entered. "Wait. I need a minute before we face whatever unpleasant surprises are waiting in there. Not that I'll be disappointed if they're not. But it would be nice to be ready for a change. Do you think you could use a power thrust if necessary?"

Jayce ran his hand through his hair. "Ummm... I guess so. Although, all you've told me is you need to be angry. Anything else I should know?"

Ellie smiled. "Well, I'm not exactly sure how it works myself. I just focus my anger on the target and kind of throw the power in that direction. If you remember, the first time it happened was an accident... and you ended up pinned to a wall."

Jayce chuckled. "I'm not likely to ever forget *that*. I remember worrying about my health if that became a regular habit. Seriously though, I was hoping to get a bit of practice at the whole power thrust thing first. Guess we'll have to hope for the best and pray I don't fold under the pressure."

"Welcome to my world. That entire trip to Jasper and Isabel's was a nightmare. I had no idea what I was doing most of the time. But at least we *both* have magic we can use now. To be honest, you've taken a huge weight off my shoulders. I definitely won't miss the pressure of being the only one who can cast spells."

Jayce pulled her to him and crushed her against his chest. "I never realised you felt so pressured. You always seem so fearless and ready to take on all comers. You were right. I sometimes felt totally useless in my ability to protect you."

Ellie sighed and snuggled closer. "I always feel safe and

protected when you're around. Hey, you know what's sad?"

He lifted her chin and smiled into her eyes. "What gorgeous?"

She reached up and touched his face. "That we have to be who knows how far underground, in some bloody great cavern full of giant wormy things, to finally have some time to ourselves. Maybe staying here isn't such a bad idea after all. Sort-of hide-out for a while. 'Far from the madding crowd' so to speak?"

Jayce chuckled and kissed the tip of her nose. "So you'd rather hangout here in a dark creepy hole in the ground full of monsters than go back to the suite at the hotel?"

"Well, at least no one here can put spells on us to keep us apart. And the wormy things are *so* easy to squish. I'd say here is the lesser of two evils, wouldn't you?"

"Well, when you put it like that..." he said, finding her lips and kissing her tenderly. "I'm suddenly seeing this place in an entirely different light."

Ellie sighed. "Yeah, well speaking of light... maybe it's reality calling. Come on... time to go home."

Ellie's sadness wrenched at his heart. She was right—it had been far too long since they weren't under pressure to either save the world, or each other, or both. And all because of one person—Thomas Raythawn.

Ellie stepped out of his arms and gripped his hand tightly in hers. "His time is coming, babe. I promise. I'm sick of always having to look over my shoulder too. And if the rebels aren't ready, we'll do it without them."

Jayce squeezed her hand. "Deal. As soon as we get back to reality, we'll start planning his downfall. But first, let's see if we can find a way to actually *get back* to reality, shall we?"

Ellie

THE LIGHT WAS the result of a beam of sunlight coming from above. Ellie tilted her head back, squinting up at its unknown source. It seemed to go on forever, so she gave up and took in the rest of the massive area. Positioned directly under the beam of light stood a large stone podium, with an open book on display. Ellie turned to Jayce and they both grinned. This was it! The Book of Time. The answers to all their questions.

They stepped toward it and all hell broke loose. Skeletal, wraith-like figures began to emerge from the walls around them, their stick-thin arms reaching out toward where the two stood.

Without hesitation, Jayce lifted his arm and released a power thrust. Ellie watched in awe as a group of the ghostly figures flew backwards, hitting the wall with such force they were once again entombed within it.

Ellie's heart hammered in her ears, her breath catching in her throat as the figures continued to pour into the cavern. *Jayce, they're coming from all sides! There's too many of them!* she screamed into his mind.

Stand behind me so we're back-to-back. And try to save your energy. Wait until a group of them are close before you use your magic.

Ellie slipped in behind him and directed a thrust at the group emerging from the wall to their left. At least half a dozen of the spectres flew backwards into the wall. But more were coming out every second. Jayce's back stayed rigid behind her, but she knew their energy would run out long before they stopped the never-ending flow.

Jayce, we need a new plan. They just keep coming. She hurled another thrust toward the wall to their right.

I'm open to suggestions. His shoulders began to slump as he sent out yet another thrust.

We need to somehow seal the walls. What if we combined our magic and energy and tried to send out a shield of some kind? She flinched backwards as one of the skeletal creatures got close enough to almost touch her. Before she could send another power thrust, something in the creature's eyes caught her attention. Sadness and pain lurked in its sunken eyes. *What were these things? Or more to the point, who had they once been?*

An overwhelming sense of what they had to do washed over her. They needed to stop fighting them. The wraiths didn't want to hurt them. She let out the breath she'd been holding, dropped her arms to her sides and smiled at the wraith hovering in front of her.

Ellie, what are you doing? Jayce's voice was tired and laced with panic.

I don't think they want to hurt us Jayce. Don't ask me how I know. I just do. I really think they're trying to tell us something?

Are you insane? Ellie, they're swarming us!

Jayce, I can't explain it. For some reason, I feel like what we're doing is wrong. Can you please just trust me on this one?

Jayce sighed and dropped his arms to his side. *I guess being sane is over-rated anyway. I trust you baby.* They both turned and wrapped their arms around each other.

"I love you. Thank you for trusting me," Ellie whispered into his ear.

"I love you more than you can possibly imagine. I'll always trust you." His warm breath on her ear sent shivers of delight through her body. She kissed him, and they waited for whatever would happen next.

CHAPTER TWENTY-THREE

Ellie

*E*llie watched Jayce's eyes grow to the size of golf balls as the wraiths turned and merged back into the walls. He shook his head.

"Damnit, Elle. How did you know? What happened?"

Ellie picked up her jaw and shrugged. "I got distracted for a second, trying to think of a plan, and realised one of them was close enough to touch me. So why didn't it? Jayce, I saw its eyes. They were so sad and filled with pain. As if they expected our reaction. That's when it hit me. What if the same thing happened to them? Somehow, I just knew we had it wrong. We needed to stop fighting them. Talk about weird... "

Jayce sucked in a breath, grabbed her hands from around his waist and held her in front of him. "Seriously? That's it? Although I suppose I shouldn't be surprised. Who else would stop fighting because they felt sorry for something trying to kill them? But I think I understand what happened now. There was never anything to fear but fear itself. If we'd continued to fight, we'd eventually have used up all our magic and energy... and we'd be dead, just like them. Thank the Stars you worked out their warning in time.

Ellie's eyes filled with tears as she finally understood the message the wraith tried to convey. Her legs turned to jelly, and she slumped to the ground, the image of those sad, haunted eyes burned into her brain. Had all those people died trying to find the Book of Time? Her heart ached for all the lost souls entombed within the walls around them.

Jayce slid to the ground beside and squeezed her hand. "At the risk of repeating myself... you are, without a doubt, the most unbelievably amazing person to ever draw breath. I can't imagine anybody else *ever* doing what you did."

Ellie's cheeks burned at his words. "Excuse me... but you did."

"Only because you asked me to stop... and to trust you. Mind you, I thought maybe you'd lost your marbles from all the stress. Every fibre in my being screamed at me to keep fighting. But I trusted you; and you saved our lives."

"Thank you for trusting me. But we saved each other. I mean, if you *had* kept arguing or asked me to explain, I probably would've changed my mind and started fighting again. I couldn't let you fight alone."

Jayce ran his hands through his hair and gave her a crooked smile. "Damn this life stuff is hard. One wrong choice, and *BAM*, you're entombed in a wall for the rest of eternity. Whatever happened to party all night and pay the price later? Although, we seem to get plenty of the 'pay the price' bit without enjoying the 'party all night' part."

Ellie smiled and sighed. She couldn't shake the memory of those sad haunted eyes. Had he died trying to read the Book? Something prodded at the back of her mind. Was there another message in those eyes? What else had he been trying to tell her? Something about the Book itself? She groaned as the answer came to her. "So, I've been thinking—"

Jayce rolled his eyes. "Oh-oh... that's never good."

She sighed and nudged him. "Shut up. I'm trying to be serious here. It's about the Book of Time—"

"Okay... you mean the Book sitting on that podium over there? The one we risked life and limb to find, and is now laying there begging us to read? That Book?"

"I *will* punch you if you don't stop," Ellie said, trying to keep a straight face. She took a deep breath and exhaled slowly. "I don't think we're supposed to read it." She held her breath, waiting for the explosion.

Jayce looked at her as if she'd lost her mind... again. "O...kay. You wanna explain *this* feeling, or is it another one of those things where I just need to trust you?"

She giggled and sighed. "It's not that hard to work out. We don't *need* the Book anymore. Just coming here and trying to find it fixed all our problems. The Book is only to be read by those who *need* its help!"

Ellie could almost see the cartoon lightbulb appear

above Jayce's head as his eyes filled with understanding. "So, if we *keep* trying, more creatures or whatever will come at us?"

"I think so, yes. So, how about we agree to just walk away, and find a way out of here?"

Jayce shrugged. "Yeah, you're right. I have to admit I was looking forward to reading some of those prophecies. But you know what they say, no news is good news."

They stood and brushed themselves off, turning their backs on the stone podium and the Book. Ellie squeezed Jayce's hand and smiled. They'd made the right decision. A sense of peace washed over her.

They only managed three steps before the walls around them began to reverberate, the sound of stone rubbing against stone almost deafening. What did they do wrong this time? Maybe she'd got the whole thing wrong, and new creatures of death were about to descend on them.

"Well played, Children of the Stars. You are indeed worthy of the blessings placed upon you by the Stars. Few survive the trials you faced and live to tell the tale. Seldom have I seen such wisdom in ones so young."

The voice seemed to be coming from the beam of light behind them. Ellie turned and eyed it warily. But nothing appeared to have changed. Jayce merely shrugged and raised his eyebrows. Since when had he become so blasé.

"Ummm... hello. Who said that?" Jayce's voice echoed off the walls of the cavern.

The rumbling started again, and Ellie's jaw dropped as she realised the voice was chuckling. "No need to yell

Jayce Raythawn. I hear everything within this cavern, even unspoken messages. I am the Keeper of the Cave, tasked by the Stars to guard the Book of Time for all eternity. I am sorry your ordeal has been painful, but this was a necessary part of the process."

Ellie frowned. "I don't understand. What process?"

"The process toward gaining the knowledge and understanding you will need to defeat the evil you must face."

Jayce groaned. "How did I guess you'd say something like that? If you're referring to yet another prophecy, I am definitely not ready to know."

"Then you would be the first to ever forego the opportunity to foresee your future. Because you survived, and passed the trials set for you, I give you a choice as your reward. You may either stay and read the Book of Time without fear of danger, or I can grant you a safe and swift passage home. Which do you choose?"

Ellie and Jayce grinned. "Home," they both said at the same time.

"You have chosen wisely. May the Stars continue to look favourably on each of you, and your union. Farewell, Children of the Stars. It has been a pleasure..."

Ellie blinked and they stood in their bedroom back at the hotel suite. They hadn't exactly teleported. The usual ground shift beneath her feet didn't happen. It was more like one minute they were in the cavern, and the next in this room. She shook her head and sighed, not interested in analysing the how's and why's any more. She was with Jayce. They were safe, home, and the curse was broken.

The door to the lounge room was closed, and Jayce immediately put his finger in front of her lips. He sat down on the bed behind them and pulled her into his lap. Ellie's heart skipped a beat. Jayce cupped her face gently between his hands and she thought she might pass out if he didn't kiss her soon. Mischief danced in the smouldering depths of his eyes.

She sucked in a breath. Conceited jerk. He *knew* she wanted him to kiss her. *Well, we'll see about that mister!* She reached up and pulled his lips down to hers, holding nothing back. She kissed him with fiery passion, drawing him in deeper, her hands slipping under his shirt to revel in the glory of touching his bare skin.

Jayce grabbed her hips and flipped her onto her back, his body trapping her beneath him. *Two can play that game you little minx.* His deep husky voice chuckled inside her head.

Yvette's voice outside the door penetrated the haze in Ellie's brain. "Promise you'll wake me in an hour, if they're not back before. I'd hate to miss—" Ellie and Jayce scrambled to sit up as the door opened. Yvette stood in the doorway, her eyes like saucers at the sight of them.

"What the...? How did you...?"

Ellie looked at Jayce and they both cracked up laughing. Totally wrong reaction considering the circumstance, but hey, she could always blame it on stress overload. She tried to pull herself together, but when the astonished faces of Jasper, Isabel and Iridia joined Yvette she laughed even harder, her stomach hurting and tears pouring down her face.

Yvette cleared her throat, and Ellie sobered at the controlled anger in her voice. "You didn't think it important to at least tell us you were back and safe? Seriously, we've been worried sick."

Jayce pulled himself together and sat up. "I'm really sorry guys. I swear, we've been back less than five minutes. Honestly, we were about to come out."

Isabel grinned from ear to ear. "Oh, give them a break. They're just kids for Stars sake. Even though they rarely get the chance to act like they are." She shooed the others out the door and turned back to look at them, gasping as she took in their filthy, blood-covered clothing. "You might want to change first." *But make it quick,* she mouthed as she pulled the door shut behind her.

CHAPTER TWENTY-FOUR

Jayce

*J*ayce dragged a reluctant Ellie out of the bedroom a couple of minutes later. He smiled sheepishly at the expectant faces of their family and friends as he sat down on the lounge and pulled Ellie into his lap. "Right, so... I guess you're all wondering how we went on Brevis?"

Jasper's face split into a huge grin. "Hell, I'm just gonna go ahead and assume things went well from what we walked in on." He winked, and the tension in the air evaporated. And then everyone was talking at once, until no one could hear what anyone else was saying over the din.

Jayce whistled and held up a hand. "Hey, everybody calm down, one at a time. You're doing my head in."

Jayce almost burst out laughing at the immediate silence following his words. They were obviously still a bit nervous about making him angry. "Will you all please stop looking at me like that? Yes, my emotions are back, but we broke the curse, so no more crazy, angry Jayce. So... I suppose we should start at the beginning..."

Jayce started to tell them everything that happened since they left, with interjections from Ellie if she thought he forgot something. When he reached the part where he fell from the staircase, he handed the reins over to Ellie. Amidst gasps and 'oh no's' she finished the story with them arriving back in the bedroom.

Yvette was the first to speak. "Okay, I need to ask about a hundred questions, but the bit about you giving Jayce his own magic is making my head spin. That shouldn't be possible!"

Ellie smiled. "Mum, you can't seriously still consider anything Jayce or I do impossible? To be honest, I think part of the reason what we do *works* is that nobody ever *told* us what's impossible. Think about it. How many people never even try because they're convinced something can't be done before they start?"

Yvette grinned at her daughter and nodded. "You just never cease to amaze me. And when did you become so wise anyway?"

Ellie giggled. "Sometimes ignorance really is bliss. Besides, it helps when two brains are working inside your head all the time instead of one."

Iridia sat forward and looked at Jayce. "So, you're, okay? The magic isn't... affecting you in any way?"

Jayce smiled. "Yes mama, I'm fine. The madness was caused by my craving for someone else's magic, not by the use of the magic itself. It was more about the addiction and withdrawals every time I *couldn't* access it."

Jasper got to his feet and crossed the room, holding his arm out to Jayce. "Well, I'm just so damned proud of you for telling us about the problem in the first place son. That madness would've eaten you up if you'd kept the secret much longer."

Jayce grabbed Jasper's wrist and smiled. "Thanks Jasper, but I'm afraid the praise should go to Ellie. She's the one who 'overheard' the thoughts inside my head and convinced me I needed help. Otherwise, I might have tried to suffer alone."

They sat around discussing various aspects of their journey for a couple of hours, a relaxed and happy atmosphere in the air. Although reluctant to spoil their well-deserved respite, Jayce couldn't get the Keeper of the Cave's words out of his head.

I am sorry your ordeal has been painful, but it was a necessary part of the process... toward gaining the knowledge and understanding you will need to defeat the evil you must face.

Time to start making plans to end this thing. Thomas had been allowed to manipulate and control the realms for long enough. He needed to be stopped. "So... I hate to be the one to ruin the party, but I think we need to start thinking seriously about our next move," Jayce said, loud enough for the conversation to end abruptly.

Yvette sighed and nodded. "You're right Jayce. So, I think it's time we stopped running and hiding and took some action. I did a lot of thinking while you two were away.

After looking at our situation from every possible angle, I'm convinced our best option is to bring the Witch Council onside first. They need to be made aware of what's been going on."

"But the members could all be tainted. They won't believe anything we say. Besides, if we try to enter the Witch Council's domain we'll be arrested on the spot," Ellie said, frowning at her mother.

"I'm sorry honey, but *we* is not part of the plan. I'm talking about *me* going to the Council and trying to convince them."

"But they've branded you a traitor too. No way I'm letting you go there alone. Who knows what they'll do to you?"

Isabel cleared her throat. "I agree with Ellie, Yvette. It's way too dangerous for you to go in there alone. We won't even know if something goes wrong."

Yvette stood and stretched, rubbing her back. "Well, I don't know about anyone else, but I'm exhausted. I was about to try and sleep earlier if you remember?" She gave Jayce and Ellie a stern look, although Jayce was sure he caught a twinkle in her eyes. He still cringed and wanted to sink into the floor.

Iridia joined Yvette and smiled at her son. "I'm with Yvette. Maybe we should all get some sleep and reconvene in the morning. "

Jayce's mouth dropped open at his mother's confidence. It had been years since he'd heard her express an opinion. Iridia saw his face and chuckled. "Thank you, both of you, for finally bringing me to my senses. It feels amazing to be free and out from under *his* power."

Jayce jumped up and hugged his mother, tears welling in his eyes. "Oh Mama, you have no idea how happy I am to see you back to your old self. I haven't seen this much life in your eyes for a very long time. I'd almost given up hope of ever seeing that again."

Iridia held him at arm's length, and a tear slid down her face. "Oh pooh, enough with the sentimental stuff now, you're making me cry. You two enjoy your dinner and get some rest. We'll call you in the morning."

The four adults filed out the door after more hugging and backslapping. When Jayce finally closed the door, he leaned back against it and blew out a long slow breath. "Thank the Stars that's over."

Ellie raced across the room and leapt into his arms, wrapping her legs around his waist. "You can say that again. I thought they'd never leave. So, what would you like to do now? Shower, eat, sleep or..."

Jayce chose the option she hadn't quite got around to mentioning.

CHAPTER TWENTY-FIVE

Ellie

*E*llie stepped out of the shower and almost passed out from the delicious smells wafting in from the lounge room. Jayce had ordered dinner! Still towelling her hair dry, she walked to the cupboard in the bedroom and spied the dress she'd bought to wear on her eighteenth birthday. The dress she never got to wear to a date that never happened.

The emerald-green sheath called to her. She smiled at the memory of her friend Sarah convincing her to buy it, 'cos she looked stunning'. How long had it been since she'd thought about her past life? The one she left in the middle of the night with no time for goodbyes. Had there really been a time when buying a new dress rated as the most important thing on her mind? She struggled to remember her life ever being that carefree.

She sighed and reached for the dress. Why not? She

might never get another chance to wear the thing, so why waste an opportunity? Slipping the dress on, she moved to the mirror, stunned by her own reflection. Her skin glowed a soft golden colour from all her time outdoors. The dress hugged her curves and accentuated her assets. She tingled all over at the thought of Jayce's reaction.

She almost chickened-out and got changed, worried she was overdressed. But she stopped and thought for a minute. This *was* a special occasion. *Her* Jayce was out there in the lounge room, and at least for tonight, they could pretend to be worry free. They were safe... and together... and whole.

She brushed her hair, smoothed the dress down nervously, and opened the bedroom door. The lounge room was in darkness, but a soft breeze came from the direction of the balcony. Rounding the corner, she sucked in a breath. Jayce stood on the balcony with his back to her. Behind him, a beautifully laid out candlelit dinner waited.

Jayce

It took Jayce less than an hour to set up Ellie's surprise dinner. He'd woken up to find Ellie sleeping peacefully beside him and decided not to wake her. He dived out of bed, bursting with energy, and jumped in the shower. Which was when he came up with the idea to surprise Ellie with a candlelit dinner. Excited by the prospect of their first real 'date', he ordered the meal and a bottle of wine, asking the waiter to set the table up on the balcony.

Satisfied that everything looked perfect, he poured himself a glass of wine and waited for his 'sleeping beauty' to wake. He leaned against the railing on the balcony, sipping on his wine as he took in the magnificent view of the harbour at night. He turned at the gasp behind him, not wanting to miss the surprise on her beautiful face. The sight of her almost made him drop his wine glass, his legs threatening to give out beneath him. *Hot damn!*

Ellie stood in the doorway wearing the sexiest damn dress he'd ever set eyes on. His pulse rate skyrocketed. He stared at her in awe, stunned by the knowledge this gorgeous, intelligent, funny, sexy woman loved him as much as he loved her.

He opened his mouth to speak, only to discover his tongue was stuck to the roof of his mouth. Heat rushed to his face, as she gave him a wicked smile. He shook his head, put his glass down on the table and reached for her hands.

He wanted to stand there and drink in everything about her for the rest of his life. *How the hell did he ever get this lucky?*

"I am totally lost for words Elle. Except... where the hell did the dress come from? It's... you're... stunning."

Ellie actually blushed and gave him with a shy smile.

His feisty, determined, stubborn sexy witch had no idea how gorgeous she was.

"So, you like it then? I bought this to wear on our first date. You know, the one we never got to go on? Better late than never huh?" A cute, breathy giggle slipped out. "Oh, and you don't look so bad yourself."

He realised her hands were shaking and pulled her into his arms. "Damn Elle... how's a guy supposed to concentrate on eating, with you sitting on the other side of the table looking like that?" She lifted her face to his and smiled.

Stars he loved her. How many times had they almost lost each other? How many more brushes with death waited around the corner? He knew she'd read his thoughts when she reached up to pull his face down to hers. She kissed him, as if she were trying to erase all the bad memories in their past. He crushed her to him, the anger and hurt wiped away. His entire body was on fire, his heart ready to burst. Before Ellie came into his life, he would never have believed it possible to love someone so completely.

A vague memory of the food going cold on the table flitted across his mind, but his appetite was gone. He wanted this moment to last forever. The worlds and all their problems, even Thomas and his evil twisted plans, ceased to exist. Ellie was everything he ever wanted and more. Nothing else mattered.

Ellie finally broke the kiss, a mischievous smile lifting her lips. "Ummm... don't you think it'd be a shame to let this beautiful meal you organised go to waste? I really think we should eat before it goes cold."

Jayce threw back his head and roared with laughter. When he could finally speak, he placed his hand on his heart and tried to assume a hurt expression. "I'm crushed! Here I am showering you with love and adoration, and all you can think about is food."

Ellie spluttered, obviously trying not to laugh. "But... but... I just wanted to make sure you knew how much I appreciated all the effort you went to!"

They both burst out laughing again, and Jayce pulled out her chair so she could sit. He ran his fingers over her bare shoulder, unable to resist kissing her gently on the back of her neck. He grinned as goose bumps broke out all over her skin. "That'll teach you to choose food over me."

Ellie was still blushing furiously when he sat down on the other side of the table. "You are *so* going to pay for that later," she said, lifting the lid off her dinner plate and sighing at the smell of roast pork. "But right now, this food deserves my full attention."

Jayce chuckled. "Yes dear."

She rolled her eyes. "Bloody hell, that sounded way too much like the response of a hen-pecked husband."

"Well, I—"

"Don't you dare! Hen-pecked my—" She stopped and grinned, cutting a piece of meat and grinning at the long-suffering face he pulled. "Nope, I'm not biting. This food is way too good. I'll sort you out later..."

They sat and bantered while they ate, soaking up the rare moments of being surrounded by 'normalcy'. His heart ached at the thought of what their lives would be like if Thomas had never been born. Just for a minute he actually considered grabbing Ellie and running away from all their responsibilities. Let someone else deal with the crap for a change.

Ellie's eyes met his and she smiled. "Pity our consciences would never let us live with ourselves. Sounds like an awesome dream though. One day babe..."

"So, you honestly believe there's a chance of having a normal life when this is all over?"

"Hey, I have every intention of growing old with you, surrounded by *our* children, and grandchildren, and great-grand—"

Jayce chuckled and raised his hand. "Okay, okay, I get it. I can feel myself aging just thinking about it."

Ellie sighed. "But before we can enjoy any of those things, we need to deal with reality. What do you think of Yvette's plan to get the Witch Council onside?"

"I agree that it's a great idea, but there's no way we can let her go in there alone. If they choose not to listen, she'll be overpowered in no time." Jayce ran his hand through his hair. He didn't want to talk about the Witch Council, or Thomas, or any of the other crap they had to deal with. But Ellie obviously needed this out of her system. She was worried about her mother.

"What if she wasn't alone? What if we went with her and hid in her house while she went to see the Council? Wait... I've got a brilliant idea."

"Elle..." Jayce growled in warning. There was no way he

was letting her put herself in danger again so soon... or *ever* again if he had his way. Damnit, they couldn't even go one whole night without talking about what they needed to do to save the worlds.

Ellie sighed and covered his hand with hers. "I'm sorry Jayce, but the sooner this is over, the sooner all this—" she waved her other hand around at the dinner and the suite behind them "—can be our reality. But until we finish what we're apparently 'destined' to do, we'll only ever be able to snatch moments of that 'normalcy' we both want."

Jayce kissed the hand he held. "Okay then little Miss Sensible... tell me about your brilliant idea."

CHAPTER TWENTY-SIX

Ellie

*E*llie studied her chewed fingernail, the conversation continuing to flow around her. The argument had been in full swing for the last twenty minutes or so, and every now and then a comment filtered into her inattentive brain. She wasn't surprised to find Yvette still stubbornly fielding all arguments against her idea to get the Witch Council onside.

Ellie tried to hide a smile. She was more like her mother than she'd realised. Once she set her mind on something... She scanned the group assembled in the lounge room and shook her head. Moving a mountain would be easier than convincing Yvette to change her mind.

"Ellie? *Ellie...* you're not even listening?" Yvette's annoyed tone penetrated the fog. "You haven't said a word. What's going on?"

"Ummm... sorry, got a bit lost in my own thoughts. I *was* listening though, sort-of. I've been waiting for everyone else to come to the same conclusion I did. You're going to the witch realm no matter what anyone says, so we just need to come up with a way to make sure you're not in too much danger."

She blushed as everyone's shocked faces told her she'd been thinking out loud. Oops, she hadn't meant to be quite so blunt.

Jasper slapped his thigh and roared with laughter. "Talk about 'out of the mouths of babes'. You hit the nail right on the head Ellie. What were we thinking, trying to talk Yvette out of anything? So, any suggestions about how we might achieve this miracle?"

Jayce chuckled and squeezed her hand. "As a matter of fact, she does Jasper. We talked about this last night, and I made her promise to wait until everyone had discussed the situation before she put her idea forward. Guess you're up, babe."

"Well, when you think about the big picture, Yvette is only in danger if we can't see or hear what's actually going on while she's inside the council meeting. And then I remembered how Jayce coughed and set the coffee table on fire when he was in human form. Jasper said it was an ability rarely heard of..."

"Anyway, that made me wonder... If Jayce can breathe fire in his human form, maybe he can use dragon speak as well. We've never tried, but since when has that ever stopped us? But if it works, everything Yvette says would be broadcast to the rest of us. But we're not sure how close to the actual meeting we'd need to be to communicate. So, what do you think?"

Jasper, Isabel, Yvette and Iridia stared at her with their mouths open. She blushed again and pretended to study her hands. "Okay, stupid idea... you don't have to say anything else."

Yvette's face broke into a huge grin. "Honey, you're brilliant! Of course, this all hinges on whether Jayce can do it... and, as you said, it depends on how far the communication will travel. What do you think Jasper?"

"I must say, I never realised how disadvantaged those of us raised in the realms are. We are so used to only thinking inside the box and restricted by what we've been told is possible or impossible, that the obvious solution never even enters our heads."

"I'm starting to think our enemies may have severely underestimated what they're up against. You, girl, are a genius!" He scratched his head and frowned at her and Jayce. "What I don't understand is why you didn't say something earlier?"

Jayce ran his hands through his hair, trying to ignore Ellie's 'I-told-you-so' look. "Ummm... well... Ellie didn't finish telling you the *whole* plan. We figured out I'll need to at least be somewhere in the witch realm to be able to communicate with Yvette."

"But, as usual, Ellie is insisting she goes too. I was just kinda hoping someone else would come up with a better plan. One that didn't involve her being anywhere near the witch realm." When no one spoke, he shrugged and shifted in his seat. "Yeah, yeah... I know... overprotective blah, blah, blah. But I had to give it a shot." He pulled Ellie closer with a sheepish smile.

Iridia beamed at her son. "Well, as a mother, I'm proud of you for trying to keep Ellie safe and out of harm's way. But honestly honey, no one's going to be safe until we finish this. And from what I've seen, Ellie's a lot tougher than you give her credit for."

Ellie almost jumped up and kissed the woman. That's *exactly* what she'd tried to tell him the night before, but he'd refused to listen. She grinned, tilting her head back to throw him her very best 'what-she-said' look. Jayce cringed and gave his mother a 'now-look-what-you've-done' scowl.

"Sorry Jayce, but I'm with your mother on this one," Yvette said. "It makes sense that you and Ellie be inside the witch realm during the meeting. If the situation starts to deteriorate, you two are probably the only ones strong enough to hold them off long enough for us to get away. Don't forget, they'll know Jayce is a dragon, so they won't expect him to be able to use magic. The element of surprise is always handy."

"So... ummm... Mum." The word still felt weird rolling off her tongue, but she knew Yvette loved hearing it. "What makes you think they'll listen to you? Thomas will have labelled you a traitor in both realms by now. What's to stop one of them killing you on sight?"

Yvette sighed. "One of my oldest and dearest friends carries a lot of influence with the Council. She's not a member, so I'm praying she hasn't been affected by the taint. If I can persuade her to have my back, I think the Council might at least grant me an audience."

"I also intend to suggest they put a truth spell on me. I'm hoping that hearing the truth about what happened to you in the Aqueous flow will convince them to question their own memories. If it doesn't work," she shrugged and smiled, "it would be a relief knowing you and Jayce aren't too far away."

Isabel, who'd sat quietly throughout the whole exchange, cleared her throat, and looked around at each of the group assembled in the lounge room. "I know this is hard for us all. No one wants to see the people they care about taking risks and placing themselves in danger. And I think we all agree that everyone in this room cares about each other deeply." Ellie's eyes filled with tears at the loving smile the older woman bestowed upon her.

"But it's going to take every resource we have to destroy Thomas. And until we do, he's made it perfectly clear he will do everything in his power to destroy Ellie and Jayce. So no matter what it takes, we need to trust and rely on each other. Now... I'm going to make coffee!"

CHAPTER TWENTY-SEVEN

Thomas

*T*homas let out an almighty roar, screwing the report into a ball and hurling it across the room. He should have squashed that damn traitor Amos and his pathetic rebels years ago. Well, they'd crossed the line this time and would pay dearly for their interference.

He paced the floor of his study, his mind screaming for revenge. He needed to come up with a plan to end this once and for all. The rebels were holed up in a fancy resort in Sydney, and whatever action he took needed to contain an unmistakable message. Thomas Raythawn would no longer tolerate traitors. The seeds of a plan began to formulate in his mind.

A strategically placed series of fires? No, they might take too long to spread and allow too many people to escape. But *bombs* might do the trick. The tragedy would more than likely be labelled just another 'terrorist attack'.

Such things were common in the mortal world, and the authorities would accept the act as yet another random protest. Perfect! That would send all the right messages to all the right people. The rebels would see the attack for what it really was, and there'd be no survivors.

And he would finally be rid of Jayce. His fists clenched and his eyes burned every time he thought about him. The ungrateful snivelling brat he once called his son had somehow managed to snatch both the witch *and* Iridia out from under him. Did the young fool honestly think he could best Thomas Raythawn, the most powerful dragon ever to exist? Well, his pathetic victory would be short-lived.

Hell yeah! This would be fun! He shivered in delight as images of the devastation the bombs would inflict flashed through his mind. He might even take the risk and be there to enjoy the fireworks. He would be like Nero, and fiddle while he watched them all burn!

CHAPTER TWENTY-EIGHT

Jayce

*N*o-one had been too surprised when Jayce managed to use his dragon voice while still in his human form. Apparently 'the adults' were finally starting to accept that the word 'impossible' didn't exist in his and Ellie's vocabulary. About damn time too!

His dragon body shivered with ecstasy as he soared through the clouds above the sparkling waters of Sydney harbour. It had been way too long since he experienced the freedom and joy of flying. The only thing missing was the feel of Ellie on his back. But he refused to let her absence put a damper on his enjoyment.

He should be sleeping, but after spending hours tossing and turning, he finally gave in to the urge to release his dragon. Ellie looked so peaceful asleep beside him he didn't want to wake her. Instead, he sneaked up to the roof and launched himself into the darkened night sky, the instant adrenaline rush telling him he made the right decision.

The upside of being alone, was not having to worry about Ellie sharing his thoughts. He loved her to death, but sometimes he needed to think things through on his own. They'd spent the entire day with 'the adults' discussing the plan for approaching the Witch Council, and in a few hours, they would be inside the witch realm. In theory, the plan appeared to cover all possible outcomes. Except that the old gut feeling Ellie had learned to rely on screamed they'd forgotten something. Something important!

So, what had they missed? He ran through the plan in his head for the gazillionth time. Yvette had paid a quick visit to Minerva, her well-respected witch friend, who'd agreed to them using her home as their base. Apparently, Minerva had also fabricated a reason for requesting an audience with the Witch Council for the following day.

Jayce would simply listen in and share the proceedings from the Council meeting with Ellie, Jasper, Isabel and Iridia. At the slightest hint of anything going wrong, he and Ellie would teleport in, grab Yvette, and get them all safely back to the mortal world. Well, that was the plan, anyway.

But Ellie's feelings were never wrong! Damnit, what the hell did they miss? He wracked his brain, and once again came up with the only possible wildcard in the plan. Trusting Yvette's old friend Minerva. What if the old witch lied about arranging the meeting? The whole thing might turn out to be a trap.

Yvette swore Minerva would never betray her, but the magical realms had changed a lot in the past few years. Jayce struggled with the idea of placing their lives in the hands of a witch he didn't know. They were taking a huge risk all landing in the home of someone who might have already betrayed them.

That must be it. The flaw in the plan. But Yvette would never accept it as even a possibility. So how did he delay everyone but him and Yvette from leaving the hotel? Ellie would never agree to staying behind if she knew what he suspected. She insisted on going with them, danger or no danger.

He'd have to ask his mother to help him. There was no other way. She could pretend to get sick just as they were preparing to leave. It might buy him enough time to check out what waited for them at Minerva's home. Ellie would be forced to stay with them, the only other one who could teleport them once Iridia felt able to travel.

Well, so much for enjoying his temporary respite as a dragon. Smoke billowed from his nostrils as he chuckled. Apparently being carefree and irresponsible wasn't something he could manage as a man *or* a dragon anymore. He banked left, realising he had no idea where he was. Probably halfway to China by now! Even the damn Stars laughed at him, twinkling cheekily as he headed back toward home.

He sped up, noticing the first faint rays of daylight on the horizon. Stars, the last thing he needed was for some mortal to look up and see a bloody great dragon in the sky overhead. Damn, he really should have slept. Oh well, no rest for the wicked as they say. But that didn't mean he couldn't slip back into bed for an hour or so and snuggle up to his gorgeous girl.

Well, you'd better not be too far off. Otherwise, that warm body you're thinking about snuggling up to might give in to the urge for coffee and get up. Ellie's sleepy voice in his head sounded so sexy he shivered and put on an extra burst of speed. He sighed with relief when the lights of Darling Harbour appeared in the distance, and he soared toward them.

You stay right where you are witch. Coffee can wait. Her tinkling laugh in his head was all the answer he needed. Being a dragon and soaring through the sky might be awesome, but he was suddenly impatient to morph back into his man form and greet the day with a certain tantalising witch in his arms.

ELLIE TRIED to pretend she was asleep when Jayce came in the door. But despite her best efforts, a giggle escaped at the thoughts running through his head. By the time he entered the bedroom she was grinning from ear to ear, sending similar thoughts right back at him.

He climbed on the bed and pinned her beneath his body. "Good morning my love," he whispered into her ear. "Sleep well?"

"Jayce... you're freezing! No wonder you wanted to

snuggle up to a warm body. Get off me before you give me frostbite!"

"Is this any way to greet your cold, weary man? The least you can do is offer to warm me up."

"Hey, you're the nutcase who decided to fly around in the middle of the night instead of staying in bed. What brought that on anyway?"

Jayce rolled onto his back and ran his hands through his wind ruffled hair, making Ellie want to kick herself for ruining the moment. But the question just slipped out. Waking up to find his side of the bed cold and empty almost gave her a heart attack.

"At least get under the blankets babe. I suppose I can grit my teeth while you use me to warm up." He lifted himself up and slid under the blankets. She shivered and pulled him closer. "So, tell me. Why the need to go flying the night before a day like today?"

Jayce sighed, his body beginning to thaw against hers. "I heard the thoughts rattling around inside your head. I know about the bad feeling, and I couldn't sleep. I thought a bit of dragon time might give me the chance to consider things from a different perspective."

"And did it?"

"Nope. As far as I can tell, we've considered every possible outcome. Do you think your bad feeling might be off for once?"

Ellie sighed. "You and I both know that's never happened before. Why would this time be any different?"

Jayce shrugged. "Your guess is as good as mine. Maybe you're gonna break a nail or something?" He chuckled and grabbed her hands before she could hit him with the pillow. Pulling her on top of him, he sobered, looking into her eyes with a smouldering intensity.

"Hey, whatever it is, we'll deal with it okay? At least your bad feeling will make us stay alert and expect the unexpected. Worrying about all the 'whatifs' will end up driving us both nuts. Let's focus on the plan and trust that the Stars have our backs." He placed a still icy hand on her bare back and chuckled as she squealed in protest. "So stop stressing and warm me up witch!"

This time the pillow came out of nowhere, and he laughed as she pummelled his face. "Okay, okay... I give up," he said, lifting his hands into the air in surrender. She stopped in mid-swing and eyed him suspiciously. Damn she was gorgeous! Taking advantage of her hesitation, he rolled them, so she was back underneath him. "How about this then?" He lowered his head until his lips almost touched hers. "Please baby... I'm freezing and I need you to warm me up."

Her eyes widened, and then she giggled. "I hate it when you use the puppy-dog eyes." She gave a mock sigh, assuming the pose of a long-suffering martyr. "I suppose so. Honestly, the things I do..."

"Lucky for both of us you love me then huh?" He caught her lips in a warm kiss. *Well, lips get cold too, right?*

CHAPTER TWENTY-NINE

Jayce

*S*till questioning himself about whether he'd made the right decision about the Council meeting, Jayce just wanted to get it all over with.

"Right, so is everyone ready to go?" He gave his mother a meaningful look, relieved to see her quick nod. He'd managed to close off his mind without Ellie noticing earlier, and his mother had begrudgingly agreed to go along with the ruse. She hadn't been happy about him walking into a possible trap—hey, he wasn't exactly over-the-moon about the idea either—but she agreed to trust his instincts and play her part.

Ellie's eyes found his and he pushed down the panic. Steeling his mind against thoughts of what might happen, he prayed to the Stars his fears were unfounded. He almost called off the whole ruse, wanting to hold her in his arms and never let her go. But her safety would always be more important than his needs.

Is everything okay babe? Ellie asked, tilting her head as a worried frown creased her brows.

His arms tightened around her of their own accord, and he pasted a smile on his face. *Yeah beautiful, I'm fine. But I'll be even better when this is all over.*

She dropped her head down against his chest, wrapped her arms around his waist, and sighed. *Me too babe.*

Jayce wanted nothing more than to pick her up, carry her back to the bedroom, lock the door and throw away the key. If anything went wrong, this might be the last time... He shoved the thought away.

"Ahem... if you two lovebirds are done, we need to get going," Yvette said with a smirk. "Good grief, anyone would think you were saying goodbye. Somehow I don't think we should keep the Council waiting."

Ellie glowed a brilliant shade of pink as they unwrapped their arms. Iridia stood to join the circle, and Jayce held his breath. He almost smiled when she staggered and put her hand to her head. Go mama! He grabbed her outstretched hand and led her back to the lounge.

"Oh, I'm so sorry. I don't know what's wrong with me. It was probably just a dizzy spell from standing up too quickly. But I need to sit for a while. You should all go and leave me here. I'm sure I'll be fine in a few minutes."

Isabel rushed to her side instantly. "Don't be silly Dia, of course we're not leaving you behind. I'm sure we can wait a few minutes until you feel better?" She turned to Yvette and raised an eyebrow.

Yvette chewed on her lip and shrugged. Jayce's heart wrenched as Ellie finally sighed and squeezed his hand. "Well, only Jayce and Yvette need to leave immediately. How about we let them go, and we can follow them in ten minutes or so?"

"But you've never been to Minerva's house. You won't be able to teleport there." Yvette said, trying to hide her relief at not having to wait any longer.

"Don't worry. I'll do what I did in the caves and teleport to wherever Jayce is. We'll be fine. You guys go and we'll catch up. Isabel, would you mind making a pot of your amazing herbal tea?"

Isabel smiled and nodded, dragging a protesting Jasper to the kitchen. "Don't even think about it old boy. You will be waiting here with us and that's final."

Jayce sent a thankful look toward his mother and gathered Ellie into his arms again. *Don't be long... I miss you already.* He tried to keep his voice calm and steady.

Ellie giggled and slapped his arm. *Oh, for Stars sake, will you just go. I'll see you in ten minutes or so.*

He kissed her forehead and moved to Yvette's side, holding her hand and closing his eyes. *I love you, beautiful girl...* and then the floor slipped away beneath his feet.

Ellie

ELLIE STARED at the spot where Jayce had been, the bad feeling so intense it threatened to choke her. She shook her head and took a deep breath, smiling at Jayce's melodramatic exit. The man was turning into a romantic sop. Not that she would ever complain. She still got the tingles every single time he gazed at her with eyes full of love. But seriously, they needed to work on the *Casablanca* style goodbye.

"I really am so sorry Ellie. I know how much you and Jayce hate being separated, and I'm the one causing it," Iridia said, reaching out for Ellie's hand and pulling her down beside her.

Ellie patted Iridia's hand and smiled. "Iridia, please stop stressing. Your son does tend to overdramatise sometimes."

Iridia's eyes dropped to her lap, but not before Ellie thought she caught a flash of guilt in the older woman's eyes. Why would she feel guilty about delaying them by ten minutes or so? No-one blamed her for being unwell.

And suddenly Ellie understood. Thomas would have made her pay for the inconvenience she caused. Years of learned behaviour was something Iridia may never recover from.

"Here we go," Isabel crooned as she placed a tray of steaming mugs on the coffee table in front of them. "Just what the doctor ordered."

Ellie sucked in a breath and grinned at Isabel. "Doctor... of course. Why didn't we think of that earlier? Iridia,

I can cast a healing spell and you'll be back on your feet in no time." The fear in Iridia's eyes made Ellie wish she could take the words back. "Ummm... only if you want me to that is? Sorry, I forget you're still uncomfortable with the whole 'everything can be fixed with magic' thing."

Iridia glanced at her watch and gave a huge sigh. Okay, this had to be about more than simply causing a delay. The woman was beside herself, and Jayce and Yvette couldn't have been gone more than five minutes. Ellie watched in horror as tears began to slide down Iridia's crumpled face.

"Oh Iridia... I am so sorry. I didn't realise magic bothered you so much. Please don't cry, we can wait as long as you..."

Iridia waved her hand in front of her face, the sadness in her eyes tugging at Ellie's heartstrings. She patted Iridia's hand again, wishing she could do something to take away her pain. Then she realised the sadness in the other woman's eyes had been replaced by fear. What the hell...?

"Ellie, I'm so sorry. Jayce begged me... I thought he'd be back by now, and we'd all be laughing at his stupid idea... he said five minutes..."

Ellie's blood turned to ice. What the hell was Iridia babbling about? Why would Jayce...? She jumped up from the lounge and glared at the three people sitting around her, her heart thumping with fear.

"Were you in on this too?" she growled, glaring at Jasper and Isabel. The hurt, confused expressions on their faces answered her question, but she was too wild to apologise. Her eyes turned back to Iridia, trying to hold back the anger and fear raging through her body. "I think you'd better explain Iridia... *right now*."

She stiffened as Jasper's hand settled on her arm. "Ellie, you need to calm down. You know better than anyone that Iridia isn't to blame for any of this. If Jayce thought you might be in danger, he would do what he felt necessary to keep you safe." He guided her trembling body back to the lounge, coaxing her to sit down. "Iridia, can you please tell us what this is all about? What's that fool boy gone and done now?"

Iridia explained what Jayce had asked her to do, her eyes flicking constantly toward Ellie, who listened in silence. When Iridia finished, Ellie dropped her face into her hands. This was all her fault! If only she'd kept her stupid thoughts about the bad feelings to herself. Then he wouldn't be somewhere in danger without her. Damn the man. She was *not* some 'damsel in distress', and she didn't need him to prove himself a hero.

Jasper sighed. "Well, it looks like Jayce's suspicions may have been right. He's not back, so we have to assume..."

"I have to go after them. This is not only about Jayce; my mother is in danger too. Did he even tell Yvette about his suspicions?"

Iridia shook her head. "He knew she wouldn't listen. So he kept his thoughts to himself."

Jasper paced the lounge room, muttering to himself and scratching his head. Finally, he stopped and met Ellie's eyes, his face haggard. "I'm sorry Ellie, but I can't let you go. Jayce did all this to keep you safe. If you go barrelling in there now, everything he did will have been for nothing. We need to find out what's happened first... *then* we'll go after them." He ground out the last words through gritted teeth, his fists clenched at his sides.

Ellie's anger slipped away, to be replaced by helpless frustration. Jayce had known exactly what he was doing. He knew Yvette would go alone if he mentioned his distrust of Minerva. Just like Ellie would insist on going with *him* if she thought him in danger. Damnit, she should have realised something was wrong from the whole 'parting love scene' thing. Jayce knew there was a chance he may never...

Nope, she wouldn't allow that thought to take root. They would find out what happened, and where Yvette and Jayce were, and bring them home. She almost choked on the sob that rose to her throat. What the hell had they ever done to deserve the crap the universe kept throwing at them? She was sick to death of crying... these people had gone too far this time. The Councils wanted her and Jayce dead because they considered them a threat? They had no idea what they'd unleashed.

Jayce

*T*o Jayce's intense relief, nothing threatening jumped out and tackled him to the ground when they arrived at Minerva's house. The old witch sat on a plush lounge chair, a tray containing a pot of tea and numerous cups in front of her. "Ah, there you are dear. Come join me. Just the two of you? I thought you said to expect more. Your daughter and some friends?"

Yvette bent down to hug the elderly witch. "One of our friends fell ill just before we left. I'm sure they'll only be ten minutes or so behind us. I brought Jayce with me so we could go through the plan while we wait."

The way Minerva 'appraised' him set-off alarm bells in his already wary mind. "Ah yes, the young dragon. Pleased to meet you Jayce."

She held out her hand in an imperial manner, as if she considered herself royalty and invited him to pay homage.

Jayce glanced at the wrinkled old hand and ignored it, nodding his acknowledgement. From the look in the old witch's eyes, her instant dislike matched his own. His jaw clenched and his hackles rose as the arrogant old cow sniffed, dismissing him as though he were nothing more than an annoying insect.

"Please, sit. I thought we'd enjoy a nice cup of tea before the excitement begins." Yvette smiled and sat down opposite Minerva. Jayce declined the offer of both the tea and a seat, thoughts of Ellie's 'bad feeling' making his gut twist. He did *not* trust this woman one bit.

But apart from their mutual dislike, everything appeared to be fine. Time to admit he was wrong. He'd just suck it up and go back to the hotel, explain about his unnecessary suspicions, and apologise for worrying them.

Man, what an idiot. Sure, he didn't like or trust Minerva, but dragons and witches had a long history of antagonistic behaviour. About to excuse himself to the two witches chatting happily, a soft thud in the next room caught his attention.

"Is there someone else here Minerva? I thought Yvette said you lived alone?" Did something flicker in her eyes? Annoyance? Anger?

"That would be my cat." Minerva almost spat the words at him, and Yvette's surprise at the scathing retort confirmed his suspicions. Whether or not what he heard was a cat, he definitely smelled a rat. Minerva attempted to make up for her curt reply as she turned an apologetic smile on Yvette. "Oh, I'm so sorry I snapped. I'm a little wound up about the meeting. You understand, don't you dear?"

Okay, now *he* had a bad feeling. *Yvette, something's wrong. We need to get out of here*, Jayce messaged to Yvette. Her eyes widened at hearing his voice in her head and she almost choked on her tea. Reaching for a serviette, she tried to conceal her blushing face as she coughed.

I think you might be right. But what about Ellie and—?

They're not coming. My mother made sure of that.

You mean you—?

Yep, just call it a hunch. But seriously, something here doesn't feel right. Minerva is way too on edge. You didn't tell her about my magic, did you?

No... she doesn't... Jayce, I don't feel well... I think... something in the tea?

Yvette toppled sideways as Jayce leapt toward her. But it was too late. Without Yvette to teleport them out of here, they were trapped. Two men emerged from each of the doors leading off the lounge room, muttering incantations as they moved toward him. Invisible bands of steel wrapped around his legs and waist, pinning his arms to his sides. He tried to morph, but whatever they were chanting must have blocked his connection to his dragon.

Who the hell were these people? Anger bubbled to the surface, his magic screaming for release. Then his brain kicked back in, stopping him from releasing the power thrust welling up inside him. Apart from being unable to use his arms, he needed to find out who was behind this before he exposed his magic. And his gut told him he should keep that particular secret up his sleeve a bit longer.

A demented cackling drowned out the loud chanting. Jayce closed his eyes and prayed his mother convinced Ellie not to come after them.

Yvette! Damnit. This wasn't just about him. His eyes flew to where she lay slumped on the lounge. Had she been poisoned or just drugged? Please Stars, don't let her be dead. Ellie would never forgive him if her mother died when he should have been protecting her.

He held his breath and focused on her body, relieved to see her chest still rose and fell. He released his breath in a sigh of relief. Yvette was alive... at least for now.

The chanting and cackling stopped abruptly, an eerie silence filling the room. He turned his head toward Minerva. Her chair was empty. An icy chill ran down his spine. He stiffened as a familiar presence moved behind him, shuddering in revulsion. He knew that rank odour. Had lived with it for years.

"Hello son," the voice grated in his ear, as pain ripped through his head. Thomas' evil laugh echoed inside his head as oblivion claimed him.

Ellie

ELLIE WANTED TO SCREAM. She stormed back and forth across the lounge room, fists clenching and unclenching by her side. Damnit, she finally understood Jayce's agony when she'd been in Thomas' castle. She was mentally exhausted from fighting against the overwhelming urge to teleport to Jayce. What if he needed her? He could be hurt or...

She closed her eyes and sighed with relief. The echo was there, keeping a perfect rhythm with her own heart-beat. Jayce was alive! Now they just needed to find him. What the hell had happened? It had been over an hour since he left with Yvette. She swallowed back a sob at the thought of her mother being in danger. She had no way of knowing whether she was...

Enough. She wanted answers ... and she wanted them now! "Stars Jasper, how long does it take to get a report from the witch realm? I could've been there and back twenty times by now!"

"I'm sorry honey. I understand how hard this must be for you, but so far no one's been able to find out anything. Everything in the witch realm appears to be normal, and the council members are denying any knowledge of a meeting being organised for today."

"What? How the hell is that even possible? Minerva told Yvette..." She sucked in a breath as the penny dropped. "Damnit, Minerva was obviously lying through her teeth. She had no intention of helping us. But why? None of this makes any sense. Why would she want to stop Yvette speaking to the council? If the council didn't believe Yvette, they could have arrested her at the meeting. We're still missing something..."

Oh Stars... no. Please no. The blood drained from her face and her legs gave out beneath her. She crumpled to the floor, wanting to curl up in a ball and cry. How could they be so stupid? Minerva had told someone about the plan. What if Thomas...?

Isabel was out of her seat and beside her in an instant. "Ellie honey, are you okay? What happened?"

Ellie tried to focus on the woman. She was so disorientated by the thoughts tumbling through her head she couldn't make the words come out. "Stars Isabel.... What if this has nothing to do with the Witch Council? What if Thomas found out about our plan to meet with them? He couldn't risk the Councils finding out about his origins, and his ability to use magic. It would make him as much a target as we are!"

Iridia gasped, her eyes filling with tears. "Oh no, if Ellie's right then Thomas has—"

"Jayce and my mother," Ellie finished through gritted teeth. "To hell with waiting Jasper, I need to get to the Witch Council. I don't care whether they believe me, or what they do to me. We have to do something before Thomas—"

Jasper growled and nodded his head. "Then I'm coming with you. I'm not letting you walk into the lion's den alone."

"Me too," Isabel and Iridia said at the same time.

She smiled at the three older dragons' intent on protecting her, and her eyes filled with tears. She desperately wanted to give in to the temptation of agreeing to accept their moral support. But she'd never forgive herself if anything happened to them. Something in her eyes must have warned them she would argue, because Iridia straightened her back and lifted her hand.

"Don't bother arguing Ellie. My son would never forgive me if I let you go alone. I may appear feeble, but I'm still a Raythawn. So my name, if nothing else, commands respect. The Council needs to hear from someone who can confirm what you're saying, and who better than the wife of the man you're condemning!"

"Well, I'll be damned," Jasper said, respect and admiration for Iridia shining in his eyes. "Iridia's right honey, about Jayce's reaction *and* the council. They'll be more likely to listen to Thomas' wife than a wanted criminal. And before you say anything else, Isabel and I are coming whether you like it or not. So... let's go give that council a piece of our minds!"

CHAPTER THIRTY-ONE

Jayce

*T*he sound of violent retching, followed by soft whimpering moans, echoed off the walls and penetrated the cloudy haze in Jayce's mind. And with awareness, came pain. He tried to locate the source of the agony radiating through his body, but it seemed to be everywhere. Just breathing made his eyes water.

A memory surfaced. Bands of steel squeezing his chest, trapping his arms beside his body. The pressure was gone, but the damage remained. His entire body ached like he'd gone three rounds with *King Kong*.

Damn. Even the simple act of opening his eyes proved impossible. Not that it mattered. From what he could see through the narrow slits, the inky darkness was the same with or without the shelter of his eyelids.

Something was seriously wrong here. His shoulder muscles burned as if someone had tried to rip his arms from their sockets. His back was pressed against a hard, rough surface... stone maybe?

The smell of damp, mould and bodily waste invaded his nostrils. He gagged, fighting back the waves of nausea and sympathising with his retching companion.

What the hell...? In another time and place, the irony of his choice of words would have been funny. Because that's exactly where he thought he might be... *hell!*

He lifted his head and almost passed out at the searing pain. The sound stopped, and he held his breath, the oppressive silence like a weight against his chest. *Whoever you are, please don't be dead.* He almost wept with relief as a soft moan came from the slumped shadow close by. Thank the Stars... his companion was still alive. The thought of being trapped alone with a decomposing body terrified him.

"Hello... who's there?" he croaked into the darkness.

"Oh Jayce... thank the Stars it's you... and you're alive." The voice choked on a sob. "It's me... Yvette...I th-thought you were dead!"

Yvette? Why was she here? He tried to move toward her, and agony ripped through his body. A dull clanking sound, like metal scraping against stone, reverberated in the silence. He froze, his blood turning to ice. Chains? Seriously?

"Yvette... I can't move. Are you chained as well? Do you know where the hell we are?" he rasped, his head spinning from the effort of forming words.

"Good question. All I know... is I woke up sick as a dog...and ch-chained to what feels like a concrete wall.

And... I can't use my m-magic. The last thing I remember... is drinking tea with Minerva?" Gasps punctuated her words as she strained to suppress the gag reflex.

Jayce winced as the memories came crashing back into his brain. Thomas' fetid stench behind him. The man's oily voice triumphant in his ear. Pain exploding in his head. Then nothing.

"Please tell me Ellie isn't here? She didn't—" His voice broke. Did he really want to hear the answer?

"No, as far as I can tell... we're the only ones here. At least, I haven't heard..." She broke off with a stifled sob. He understood what she meant. She didn't think there was anyone else here *alive*. "Jayce? Did... did you see what happened? Any idea where we might be... or how we got here?"

"Thomas," he said flatly, bile rising up into his throat at the bitter taste of the word on his tongue. Yvette groaned, and then the retching started again. His head slumped forward onto his chest.

Why the hell hadn't he shared his suspicions with the others? Ellie's bad feelings were never wrong. Because he was an arrogant idiot! Too busy playing the hero as usual. He'd thought he could handle the situation, and instead he let Yvette walk blindly into a trap.

"Jayce." Yvette's shaky voice was hardly more than a whisper. "I remember your voice in my head just before I passed out. Something about your mother stopping Ellie from following us. So what aren't you telling me?"

"Bloody hell, Yvette. I stuffed up... big time. This is all my fault. Ellie got one of her really bad feelings about the plan, and I thought I had everything under control." He shuddered and confessed everything. From when he first decided to act on his suspicions, to the last thing he remembered. Thomas' sick voice in his ear. "I'm so sorry Yvette..."

Yvette moaned softly. Jayce held his breath, waiting for the tirade of abuse he deserved. Yvette had every right to be angry with him. He hung his aching head in shame, wishing he was dead.

"You know the saddest part?" The lack of anger in her voice surprised him. "You're right; I wouldn't have listened. So, I'm just as much to blame for our situation as you. Except that I'd probably have dragged Ellie and the others along with us. Thank you for thinking of Ellie's safety above all else... again. I'm so glad she has you in her life."

And then she finally broke down and sobbed. Jayce's heart went out to this woman who'd suffered so much heartache in her life. She didn't deserve any of this.

His anger surfaced through the pain, roaring to life at the injustice! How dare Thomas put them all through this! He treated people like pawns in a game, using and discarding them on a whim. He would be waiting for Ellie to come to their rescue.

Jayce sent a prayer to the Stars, begging them to stop her from doing what Thomas expected. He remembered his own frustration when Thomas had taken Ellie. Hell, not going after her had nearly killed him! She would be feeling the same. But their friends had stopped Jayce from playing into Thomas' hands, and he prayed Ellie would listen to them.

Yvette had gone silent, her sobs reduced to shuddering breaths "Don't worry Jayce. I'm sure Jasper, Isabel and your mother will talk her out of coming after us," she said, as if she could read his thoughts. "Besides, she knows how Thomas thinks. I'm sure she'll come up with a plan to get us out of here. And if not, at least she's safe." She surprised him again when a soft chuckle floated on the air towards him. "Damnit, I was *so* looking forward to grandchildren!"

Jayce was speechless. Yvette had come to the same conclusion as him. Thomas wouldn't hesitate to dispose of them both as soon as they reached their 'use-by' date. Ellie... marriage... children... happily ever after. A tear trickled down his face as he felt them all slipping away.

CHAPTER THIRTY-TWO

Ellie

*E*llie stepped through the front door of the Witch Council headquarters with her head held high. She was both relieved and disappointed to find the place just as deserted as the last time she was there.

She had no idea what she was going to say or do when she found someone. But she would at least *appear* fearless. This fiasco had gone on way too long, and it was time someone talked some sense into these useless idiots.

She stiffened as someone stepped out of a doorway and hurried down the hallway towards them. She tried to hide a grin as she recognised the witch her and Yvette encountered on their last visit. She remembered wanting to slam the old hag up against a wall. Maybe the witch wouldn't be so lucky this time.

"Who are you, and what are you doing here? These are

the Council's private chambers. Best you be turning around and going back where you came from or I'll—"

Ellie stepped right up to the woman's face, her eyes blazing with fury. "...or you'll what? Huh?"

Iridia's gentle hand on her shoulder reminded her why she was here. Ellie sucked in a deep breath and took a step back. "Look, whoever you are, I need you to call an urgent Council meeting immediately. It's a matter of life or death."

The hag's previously haughty attitude became cautious. "And who are *you* to be demanding the Council convene on such short notice?"

"Well, I suppose you wouldn't remember me from the last time I was here. I may have appeared a little... older. But I believe you know my mother, Yvette Fiora. And I'm quite certain the Council will be interested in what I have to say."

The woman's mouth flapped open and closed a few times before she vanished. Ellie chuckled. "Okay, I think that got their attention. Let's go down to the meeting room and wait for them to come flocking in."

Iridia moved to walk beside her as she strode down the hallway, toward the room she'd visited twice before without ever meeting a Council member. "Ellie, I'm sorry I interfered. I assume you had a previous run-in with that witch, but now is not the time or place for paybacks."

Ellie pulled Iridia's arm through hers, patted her hand and smiled. "No need to apologise Iridia. You're absolutely right... she'll keep."

They walked in a companionable silence, Jasper and

Isabel following closely behind them. Ellie pushed the door of the meeting hall open and smiled at the surprised looks on the faces of the witches in the room. They hadn't expected her to know her way around.

"Good morning. Please don't bother trying to come up with a plan to incapacitate myself and my friends. I assure you the shield protecting us is way beyond your ability to disarm."

"So... I believe you've been told who I am? I've come here today to straighten out a few misconceptions, and I think it would be in your best interests to sit, listen and not interrupt until I'm finished."

A chorus of angry voices filled the air.

"Who the hell..."

"Of all the..."

"How dare you..."

Ellie grinned at all the expected responses, until her eyes found the witch she'd been looking for. The intense curiosity in the woman's eyes told her *this* was the one she needed to convince. Ellie tilted her head and raised an eyebrow. She could've sworn the old witch's lip twitched, as if trying to suppress a smile. The woman held up a hand and the babble ceased.

"You heard the young lady. I suggest we all take a seat and listen to what—Ellie is it?" she nodded. "—what Ellie has to say. I am Helena, the Chairperson for the Witch Council. Personally, I can't wait to hear this story. I assume your friends are here to support your arguments?"

Ellie waited until the witches were all seated. She'd remembered the circular room, and deliberately planted herself and her friends in the middle. There was bound to be at least one witch in this room in cahoots with Thomas, and they would be ready.

"Thank you, Helena. Yes, allow me to introduce you to my dragon friends. I'm sure you are all familiar with Thomas Raythawn, the Chairperson for the Dragon Council. This is his wife Iridia Raythawn." Ellie ignored the murmured whispers. "And my dear friends Jasper and Isabel White, who were declared rogues five years ago by Thomas Raythawn for fabricated reasons."

Helena quickly silenced the shouts of outrage from some of the council members. Ellie smiled her thanks, surprised by the twinkle in Helena's eyes. The shrewd old witch actually seemed to be enjoying herself!

"So... I suppose I should start at the beginning..." Ellie began her story with the random meeting between her and Jayce, and the unexpected, and unwanted, creation of their bond as witch and familiar.

She found herself reliving the events as the story unfolded. By the time she reached the part about the Tree of Life being poisoned, and their own personal self-sacrifices to save the Tree, she knew she held the undivided attention of the entire Witch Council.

She winced as she related what had happened inside the Aqueous flow. Tears threatened to spill out as she explained how the taint warped and twisted their memories until they couldn't tell the truth from the lies.

She lifted her chin and stared directly at Helena. "Jayce and I were able to break through the effects of the taint because of our love for each other, and the strength of the bond between us. It wasn't until later that we wondered if others may have been affected by the taint. When did the Witch and Dragon Councils last meet on Brevis?"

Helen appeared startled by the question. Ellie glanced around at the other witches in the room and saw the same confusion on their faces. "Well, I'm not sure exactly. Perhaps a year ago?"

"And did anyone's... behaviour... change noticeably after this event?"

"As a matter of fact, I seem to recall a few problems started about then. But wait, are you suggesting the Council members may have been exposed to this taint?"

"Well... I'm hoping *you* might be able to tell *me* if it's possible. Can you think of any cases where a Council member's behaviour became irrational and out of character following the visit to Brevis?"

From the whispering among the Council members, Ellie knew she'd triggered a memory or two with that question. She waited patiently for the old witch to elaborate.

Helena cleared her throat, looking distinctly uncomfortable. "There have been a few random incidents over the last couple of months that could be explained by this taint you're referring to."

"Perhaps it would be best at this time for you to continue with your story. I'm unwilling to discuss the matter further until I'm convinced you can be trusted."

Ellie sighed and nodded. "Fair enough, can't say I blame you. I'd probably do the same thing in your shoes. Now where was I...?"

Ellie continued, relating the details of their encounter with the Lord of the Lake and their consequent return to the mortal world. She described the process they'd used for restoring the Tree of Life and paused to take in the reactions of the Council members. This was where she expected it to get interesting. Jasper, Isabel and Iridia were on high alert for any unusual behaviour from the Council members. Exposing Thomas' involvement was sure to elicit a strong reaction from his supporters. She took a deep breath and continued.

"Once restored to her former glory, the Tree of Life revealed the identity of the person who'd attempted to destroy Her and annihilate the entire mortal race. At first, she referred to him as the Dark Lord... But he is better known as Thomas Raythawn, Chairperson of the Dragon Council." Stunned silence followed her words.

"But by far the most surprising news was that of his lineage. The Tree described the Dark Lord as being of both witch and dragon blood. It seems Thomas Raythawn is the product of the ill-fated union between the witch and dragon bonded hundreds of years ago. His mind is twisted by his insatiable hunger for power and revenge, and he and his followers have resorted to the use of dark magic. His intention is to overthrow the Councils and reign supreme. And he will happily destroy anyone who gets in his way."

CHAPTER THIRTY-THREE

Jayce

*P*ain had become his constant companion. Jayce had no idea how long they'd been imprisoned in their dark tomb... time had ceased to exist. He welcomed the icy numbness as it settled over his broken body. Better to feel nothing.

The last visit from 'the animal', the name he'd given the man who derived such pleasure from inflicting pain, had been the third since they arrived— and the worst yet. He should have realised something was wrong when the animal commented on the state of his and Yvette's parched lips, his face twisting into an evil leer as he picked up a water bottle from beside him. Surely the man didn't intend to give them water?

The hose appeared in the man's hand out of nowhere, the icy blast cutting into his skin like knives. He tried to curl into a ball, but the short chains attached to the manacles at his hands and feet prevented the necessary move-ment. Instead, he closed his eyes and gritted his teeth, sucking as much of the blessed liquid into his mouth as possible.

When Yvette started to scream, Jayce hurled insults at the animal in an attempt to draw the punishment away from her, until he passed out.

"Jayce?" Yvette's croaky voice penetrated the pain-filled haze. "Jayce... can you hear me? Please... I don't want... to be in here alone."

"I'm okay," he rasped. "How're you doing?" He licked the last of the water droplets from his lips, trying not to heave as the warm coppery taste hit his tongue. It was liquid, and his body needed it.

"Thank the Stars! I thought... he killed you." The slight hiccups in her voice told him she'd been crying. He searched his cloudy brain for words to dispel some of the despair.

"Well, at least the shower made the place smell a bit better," he said, unable to summon the chuckle he wanted to add. He sighed and closed his burning eyes. "Yvette, we can't give up. Ellie needs us to survive. She can't beat Thomas alone."

Yvette sucked in a breath. "How do you do that? How do you always manage... to 'look on the bright side', even in the midst of despair?"

"I had a good teacher. As far back as I can remember, Thomas did everything in his power to break me. It just made me all the more determined never to let him win. I guess I just trained my brain and my emotions to switch off to the negativity and find something positive to hold onto. As I got older, it became a form of self-preservation. It used to drive Thomas crazy." This time a harsh wheeze surfaced from his dry throat. It was about the closest thing to a chuckle he could manage.

"I can't even begin to imagine how hard it must have been to grow up living with that monster. I'm sorry you and your mother had to endure that."

In a way, it was a blessing the darkness hid the state of their battered bodies from each other and themselves. *Seeing* what they looked like would have increased the despair a hundredfold. If Thomas had realised his error, their cell would be ablaze with lights, mirrors covering every wall.

He froze at the sound of a door opening, the thump of heavy boots announcing the arrival of 'the animal'. How long had it been since his last visit? Jayce squinted as a figure approached, the sudden light in the darkness like hundreds of needles penetrating his brain.

"Well, well, well, *son*. I trust you're finding your accommodation suitably uncomfortable?" Jayce couldn't decide whether to be relieved or terrified at the sound of Thomas' gloating voice.

"Seems the only thing we're missing here at our little get-together is your morwitch slut. Although I'm certain the disappearance of her mother and her lover should guarantee a predictable and useless rescue attempt. Actually, you should pray she doesn't arrive too quickly. Because, as I'm sure you've already guessed, once I have her, there'll be no need to keep you alive any longer. Her arrival will mark your death. A fitting end to our battle, don't you think?"

"I am not your *son* Thomas. I thank the Stars every day that your blood doesn't flow through my veins. I swear to the Stars that I *will* kill you. You're a monster and need to be put down like any other rabid animal."

"Brave words for someone totally powerless and chained up in the dark. Tell me, did you enjoy the visits from my good friend Boris? He's very... adept... at what he does, wouldn't you agree? He was most unhappy when I told him to retrieve the morwitch from her dithering old aunts' place and bring her to me *unharmed*. I promised him I'd make it up to him, and you and her dear sweet mother provided me with the perfect solution."

Thomas held the light up close to the bars of their cage, running a dispassionate eye over their mutilated bodies. "I'm pleased to see his skills weren't diminished by the wait."

"You won't get away with this. There'll be questions about our disappearance."

Thomas harsh laughter echoed off the stone walls. "You mean the useless old dragons who've been helping you? My wife included? I must say, I was disappointed when she didn't arrive for the meeting. I was eagerly anticipating our happy reunion."

"You'll never get your hands on her again. She is safe, and no longer has to put up with your abusive insanity. I'm done talking to you monster. The stench of your evil makes me sick."

"You don't dictate the terms here. You'll be done

talking when I say you're done!" Thomas' voice was high pitched and filled with venom. Jayce smiled. He'd managed to get under Thomas' skin. Just like old times, except Thomas didn't have Iridia here to take it out on.

Thomas sucked in a deep breath and the controlled mask slipped back into place. He rubbed his chin and chuckled, tilting his head as an evil grin spread across his face.

"Goodness, all this chit-chat almost made me forget the reason for my visit. I have a surprise for you. I so hope your morwitch slut and my treacherous wife are holed up safely in that resort in the mortal world. I'm looking forward to spending the evening watching the place turned into a pile of rubble. What do you say to that, huh?"

Jayce heard Yvette's gasp, and he steeled himself against revealing the impact of Thomas' words. The maniac was going to blow up The Majestic! Jayce ground his teeth together, straining to maintain the mask of indifference on his face. He refused to acknowledge the other man's presence. He said he was done talking, and he wouldn't give Thomas the satisfaction of a response.

"I asked you a question, son," Thomas spat. "What no more threats?"

Silence hung in the air, and Jayce derived the tiniest bit of pleasure from defying him one last time. The bastard wasn't going to have it all his way. He could go to hell!

"You think I don't know what you're doing? Perhaps an extra visit from Boris will loosen your tongue!" he ground out, the spittle flying from his mouth making him look even more like the feral animal Jayce had accused him of being.

Once again, Thomas pulled himself together and grinned. "Now I must be off... wouldn't want to be late for the fireworks. Hopefully the next time we meet I'll bring you a couple of new roommates... although they may be in slightly charred bits. But I'm sure you'll recognise the remains."

Thomas turned, the sound of his heavily thudding boots receding into the distance. Jayce waited for the last remnants of light to disappear before his shoulders slumped and he allowed his tightly suppressed emotions free rein.

He opened his mouth to scream, but instead of sound ripping from his aching throat, a burst of energy blossomed deep in his belly, and a stream of fire hit the stone wall in front of him, illuminating the stunned expression on Yvette's battered face.

CHAPTER THIRTY-FOUR

Ellie

*E*llie had almost finished her long tale for the Witch Council and was surprised there'd been no sign of an attack. Maybe none of the Witch Council were Thomas' supporters after all. Who knew eh?

"Ellie... to your left," Jasper yelled. But Ellie had already seen the witch rising to her feet, her face a mask of hatred.

"Kill the morwitch! It's all lies!" the witch screamed, raising her arm and directing a power thrust at Ellie. The magic bounced harmlessly off the shield she'd erected around them. Before the screaming witch could recover from her shock, Helena raised her hand, pointed, and immobilised her.

Ellie caught the looks of awe and confusion on the faces of the witches in the room. She doubted any of them had the slightest idea how to erect a shield. She chuckled to herself. Lucky she'd found that spell and perfected the art of casting it before she left home.

But she had no interest in the other witches. Only Helena's reaction was important. Ellie's instincts told her that Helena alone possessed the power to reverse the death warrants currently hanging over their heads, and to convince the Council to help them.

"Well, no surprise there. I knew if Thomas had a sympathiser on the Council, she wouldn't be able to stop herself from defending his 'good name'." She held Helena's gaze and raised an eyebrow. "If it's alright with you, I'll be needing to extract some information from her once you've heard the rest of my story."

Helena nodded, and the woman was removed from the room. "Please continue... Something tells me there'll be a lot more surprises before you're finished."

"You have no idea," Ellie said, again holding the old witch's gaze. She continued with her story, her eyes burning as she described the destruction of her home. Taking a deep breath to steady herself, she recounted the tale of her abduction by Thomas. Shock, anger, and sympathy were all evident on the old witch's face as she listened intently.

"And this is where my dear friend Iridia's involvement began. She risked the anger and certain punishment from her husband to help me get away. She can corroborate everything I've told you regarding Thomas' duplicity and crimes."

Helena gave Iridia a sympathetic look, and then

frowned. "May I ask why your mother, and your dragon familiar aren't with you today?"

"Oh, don't worry... I'm getting to that," Ellie said through gritted teeth. A harsh strangled laugh escaped her throat. "It's the reason I decided to throw caution to the wind and come here today. Jayce and Yvette have disappeared. They came to the witch realm earlier today, supposedly to attend a meeting with the council and ask for your help in stopping Thomas. I'm just going to go ahead and assume they never made it to that meeting?" Helena's obvious surprise and lack of knowledge on the matter confirmed her suspicions.

"Then it's as we thought. Thomas has them. And he's waiting for me to come to their rescue so he can be rid of us once and for all." She shrugged and looked at Helena.

"We're not the enemy. We never were. Thomas played on the paranoia and fear caused by the taint to convince the Council members to hunt us down. He knows the power Jayce and I share through our bond is the only threat to his plans. And unless we trust each other, and agree to work together, he'll win."

Ellie held her breath and sent a silent prayer to the Stars. She'd given it her best shot. Now it was up to the Witch Council, or more specifically Helena, to decide whether they would follow through with the death warrant or help them to free Jayce and Yvette. She decided at the last minute not to reveal Jayce's magic yet. If the Council agreed to help them, she would tell Helena. Otherwise, *that* information would remain a closely guarded secret.

Helena rose from her chair and crossed the room. Opening a door Ellie hadn't previously noticed, the witch indicated for them to enter the room behind it. "This is my office. I will personally guarantee your safety while-ever you are within the council grounds, regardless of the outcome of this meeting. The Council will need to convene in private to discuss what we've learned and vote on where we go from here. I understand that time is short and will endeavour to expedite the process." Helena's eyes met Ellie's as she passed her, and something in the other witch's eyes told her they already had her vote. Hope blossomed in Ellie's chest.

As soon as the door closed behind them, Ellie's trembling knees gave way, and she slumped into a chair. The act of appearing confident had been both exhilarating and draining. Jasper, Isabel and Iridia looked at her in awe, and she smiled a sheepish smile. "So how did I do? Do you think we got through to them?"

Isabel wrapped her arms around Ellie's shoulders and kissed the top of her head. "You were absolutely amazing. I couldn't be prouder if you were my own daughter. And I know your mother and Jayce would be too."

Ellie's eyes filled with tears at the mention of Jayce and her mother. She shuddered at the thought of what Thomas could be putting them through, while she sat here in comfort and safety. Hell, they may not even still be alive!

She closed her eyes and focused on finding the echo, her heart plummeting when she located the feeble echo. It was almost as faint as when he'd been hurt and dying in the cave. Dear Stars, Jayce needed her help *now*, and she didn't know what to do. How could she help him without walking into Thomas' trap and killing them all?

An idea entered her frantic brain, and she prayed to the Stars it would work. Focusing on an image of his warm, golden eyes, she began to chant in her mind.

I love you Jayce... my energy is yours to use for as long as you need it.

She repeated the words over and over in her head, tears pouring down her face as she willed him to take what he so desperately needed. Her eyes widened as she felt the energy seeping from her body. It was working! She continued to chant until she had nothing left to give, before slumping to the floor unconscious.

CHAPTER THIRTY-FIVE

Jayce

*J*ayce sat in stunned silence as he watched the glowing embers on the wall fade away.

"What the...? Jayce, how the hell did you do that?" Yvette croaked.

Jayce shook his head in confusion. "No idea. I'm just as shocked as you are, believe me. But if I had to guess, I'd say Ellie just transferred her energy to me. I don't know *how* she did it, but it's the only thing that makes sense."

"She what? How—?"

"We did it once before, in the cave. Ellie was too weak from healing me to deal with the wormy things, so I tried to gift my energy to her, and it worked. Just like she gifted her magic to me. Stars Yvette, I don't know how she did it without us being together, but the energy literally flooded into me."

"But I still don't understand how you released fire.

Surely your magic is bound like—?" She sucked in a breath.

"Thomas doesn't know..." they both said at the same time and began to laugh. A harsh, broken, rasping laugh, but definitely a laugh.

Jayce sighed, feeling like an idiot for not thinking to use his magic before now. "So, lucky you know all the words to the spells we're going to need to get out of here. How about we start with one that'll remove these chains? Then we'll see whether I'm strong enough to reverse the spell binding your magic. After that, we should organise a surprise for our old friend Boris."

"Sounds good to me," Yvette said, the relief in her voice making him smile. "But first, some light I think..."

He repeated the spell she gave him, conjuring a small globe of light against the darkness. He groaned when the spell to open the manacles took effect. The pins and needles from the blood rushing into his numbed hands was almost unbearable. Yvette started to sob again, but he was almost certain they were tears of relief this time.

"Deep breaths, Yvette. We're almost there. Now say a prayer to the Stars I have enough power to unblock your magic. What's the spell?"

Seconds later, Yvette gasped and told him the spell had worked. His eyes filled with tears, gratitude for Ellie's gifts making his heart ache. They sat in silence for a few minutes, stunned by the knowledge that their escape might finally be achievable. He smiled when Yvette fetched a couple of bottles of water, rolling one across the floor to him.

"You need to sip, slowly," she warned. "Even though every fibre in your body will want to gulp it down."

Jayce nodded, and forced himself to take small sips, savouring the glorious relief to his parched throat. He was sure water had *never* tasted so good.

"Okay, so my body is absolutely screaming to be healed, but I don't want Boris to realise anything's changed. Not until he's opened the damn cage and about to lay in the first boot."

Rage thundered through his veins at the thought of giving the animal a taste of his own medicine. He wanted to rip the man limb from limb. But if he gave his rage free rein, he was no better than the 'animal' who got off by inflicting pain on others.

Jayce gritted his teeth and swallowed back the bile in his throat as he took stock of his 'Boris inflicted' injuries. From the sharp pain every time he took a breath, a couple of ribs were cracked. And his face felt so swollen he suspected a few other broken bones in the jaw, cheek, and nose area.

Then there were his hands. Boris had derived a great deal of enjoyment from grinding them into the stone with his boots. Yvette's cries, pleading for him to stop, only increasing his excitement.

"Yvette," he ground out, his voice harsh in his ears. "I need you to decide how we should handle Boris. Otherwise, I'm afraid I won't be responsible for my actions."

Yvette nodded. "I understand. And I'm proud of you for recognising what that retaliation would do to your own soul. Don't worry, Boris will pay for what he's done.

Knowing Thomas as we do, I'm certain he'll inflict his special brand of punishment on the man when he discovers we escaped while under his watch. All *we* need to do is leave him here defenceless and imprisoned. What do you think?"

Jayce chuckled. "I think you have a very devious and clever mind. But do you think we could hurt him just a little?"

JAYCE'S HEART raced at the sound of Boris returning for his next visit. Jayce shuffled back to where his chains and manacles lay against the wall and doused the small globe of light. Instead of the dread and fear that usually washed over him at the sounds of Boris' imminent arrival, a thrill of pleasure ran through Jayce's battered body. His mind screamed for revenge, but he locked the desire away, determined to preserve his sanity and sense of self-worth. He would be the better person and control his emotions, even if it killed him.

Boris chuckled as he placed his lantern on a side table and pulled out the key-ring. "Did ya miss me? I had to wait for his Lordship to leave for t'night's celebrations before I could pleasure youse with another visit. He's real excited about the fireworks ya'know. I hope yer loved ones appreciate all the trouble he's gorn to."

He swung open the door and stood in front of Jayce

with his hands on his hips, taking a moment to inspect his handiwork. Jayce kept his eyes glued to the man's boots, knowing if Boris saw the excitement in his eyes they'd lose the element of surprise. Boris was a powerful mage in his own right, and they needed to make sure he was immobilised before he suspected anything.

"What? Cat got yer tongue?" he said, shuffling his feet in anticipation of where he'd land the first kick. Jayce let the anger build, waiting for the right moment to release the power thrust. "Is that any way to greet a friend?"

Boris lifted his boot and swung backwards. "Not this time pig," Jayce yelled as he threw his arm out and directed the thrust at the man's chest. Boris' eyes widened with shock as he flew backwards and thudded into the stone wall beside Yvette. She chanted the spell to bind his magic, and it was all over.

Jayce grinned in satisfaction. He'd heard the cracking of bones as the man impacted with the wall, before sliding to the ground in a crumpled heap. Jayce's only regret was that he wouldn't see the man's face when he woke up.

"Damn that felt incredible," Jayce said, agony burning through his face at the grin he couldn't hold back. "Now, I think some healing is way overdue. Time we got back on our feet and out of this rat-hole. Wherever Ellie is, I can take us there. But something tells me she wouldn't cope with us turning up in this state."

CHAPTER THIRTY-SIX

Ellie

*E*llie opened her eyes to find Jasper, Isabel and Iridia hovering around her. Damn, had she seriously fainted? Memories of the energy being slowly drained from her body made her sit up in excitement, the resulting dizziness and nausea telling her it wasn't the best idea she ever had.

"Here, steady on girl." Jasper reached out to support her, his voice soft and gruff. "But now you're awake, you'd better start explaining what the hell just happened. You scared the bejesus out of us."

Ellie chuckled. "Yeah, sorry about that. I heard Jayce's echo, but it was so weak I panicked. I remembered how he sent me his energy in the cave, and just focused on pushing mine toward him. I didn't even think it would work. But then I started feeling weaker, so I knew he was getting it." She couldn't hold back the huge grin spreading across her face. "So, I think we can safely assume he got it. How long was I out? Did I miss anything?"

"Almost an hour," Isabel said, pushing Jasper out of the way to offer Ellie the glass of water she held. "I've been worried sick. I was about to call Helena in and insist she heal you." She blushed and sighed. "Oh, and no, Helena hasn't been back yet. I think she might have a fight on her hands with some of the other members."

Iridia cleared her throat and reached for Ellie's hand. "So, you felt Jayce through your bond?"

"Yeah, but only just. By the time I thought to check... But at least he was still alive. I'm hoping the energy I sent him kept him going long enough to—"

"Sure did, my beautiful angel." Jayce's raspy voice drifted across the room. Ellie's heart skipped a beat, and her breath froze in her throat. *Please, please, please tell me I'm not hallucinating?*

The speed at which the heads of the three people surrounding her swivelled to the other end of the room answered her question.

Jayce was here... alive... and safe!

Ellie tried to jump off the lounge and throw herself at him, but her legs refused to play the game. Jayce moved like lightning, scooping her up before she hit the ground. Being back in his arms was like floating on a cloud. Had he really only been gone a day? It seemed more like an eternity...

She ran her fingers over the familiar contours of his face, gasping as she recognised the yellow tinge of faded bruising. He'd obviously healed himself, but the damage must have been horrific to still show traces of abuse.

"Ahem, yes thank you darling, I'm fine too. Thank you so much for asking..." Her mother's voice floated over her shoulder.

Ellie turned, horrified by her lack of concern for her mother. She relaxed when she saw the teasing twinkle in Yvette's eyes. "That's okay sweetheart. You look exhausted. I'm assuming the state you're in is a result of sending Jayce too much energy?"

Ellie blushed. "I-I couldn't tell whether he was getting it or not. So I just kept going until I couldn't anymore."

Jayce frowned down at her. Fear, anger, and love battling in his golden eyes. "Elle, you could've killed yourself." He sighed and rested his head against hers. "I know what you do is always for the right reasons, but seriously babe, you need to be more careful."

"Can you two please quit picking on me and show some damn gratitude? And maybe you should all stop standing around being such damn sour-faced worry-warts and get on with the celebrating. You're both here, and you're safe, and that's all I care about."

The door to the office opened and all heads turned. Helena stood in the doorway beaming. "I have some excellent news. The Council—" Her eyes widened as she took in the scene before her. "Yvette? How did you...? And I assume this is Jayce, your dragon familiar Ellie?" Helena groaned and shook her head. "Honestly, you people are going to be the death of me. How the hell do I explain to the Council that the two people they finally agreed to help rescue are now standing in my office?"

Yvette stared at them with her mouth open. "You were going to help us escape? I swear, this has been the weirdest day of my life."

Isabel stepped forward and beamed at the group of confused, tired, happy people in the room. "Hmmm... I can't decide whether tea or coffee would be better. Any preferences?" she asked, managing to maintain the deadly serious expression on her face as those around her cracked up laughing. She shrugged, the corners of her mouth twitching. "Fine, I suppose I can make both. Helena, where's the nearest kitchen?"

Jayce

JAYCE WAS STUNNED to learn he and Yvette had only been gone a day. With the darkness in the cell, and them both dropping in and out of consciousness, time had lost all meaning. Rage ripped through his body again. So Boris must have beaten and tortured them at least every hour. The man's insane desire to cause pain made Jayce want to vomit.

He heard a gasp from Ellie and wanted to kick himself. All colour drained from her face. *Damnit!* He'd let the images of what Boris did to them surface in his head, forgetting she would see and feel every detail. Big fat tears rolled down her face as she stared at him in horror.

He pulled her into his arms, slamming the door to his mind closed and pushing the rage back down into its cage. "I'm so sorry Elle. You were never supposed to see any of that."

"J-Jayce... the man. He was the one—"

"I know sweetheart. His name is Boris, and he bragged about being the one who grabbed you from the aunts' kitchen. I wanted to rip the animal limb from limb."

"Thank the Stars you got the energy I sent, and that it helped. I was terrified when I felt how weak you were."

"I must admit, discovering I had the energy to slam that animal against a stone wall was like winning the lottery. The only thing better was seeing the shock in his eyes. Nothing short of spectacular."

Jayce cast a glance toward where Yvette and Helena sat huddled in a corner talking quietly. Helena gasped, and he assumed Yvette had told her about Thomas' plans in the mortal world. Helena pushed her chair back, wringing her hands in front of her. Her eyes met Jayce's across the room. He nodded, as if to confirm what Yvette said, and she jumped to her feet.

"We need to stop him. He's insane!" Helena paced back and forth in the crowded room.

Jasper stood up, putting his hands on his hips. "Stop who? Thomas? What's he done now?"

Yvette turned to Jasper, her eyes filled with pain. "He's planted bombs at The Majestic in Sydney, and he's gone to watch the fireworks. We don't know what time they're set to go off, only that it will be tonight." Tears streamed down her mother's face. "He thinks you're all still there. He plans to take everyone out in one hit."

Ellie's face was deathly pale. "But hundreds of innocent people will be killed. We have to do something!"

Helena lifted a hand for silence, her commanding presence restored. "It's going to take more than just those in this room to locate and disarm the bombs in time. We're going to need the full support of the Council. Are we ready to go out there and convince them?"

Ellie shot to her feet. Jayce tried to hide a smile as she wobbled from her depleted energy. *Damn she was amazing.* His heart swelled with pride as his feisty girl prepared to do battle with the staid, indecisive Witch Council. He stood and slipped a supportive arm around her waist. The least he could do was give her back some of the energy she almost killed herself sending him.

She smiled and squeezed his hand, acknowledging and accepting his support. She turned fiery eyes on the rest of the group.

"So why are we still sitting around talking about it?"

CHAPTER THIRTY-SEVEN

Ellie

*E*llie chewed her lip as she took in the crowds milling around them, stunned by the amount of people overflowing from every available café, bar and night spot.

Of course there'd be people everywhere. It was a Saturday night in Darling Harbour. She looked sadly at The Majestic resort sprawled at the other end of the esplanade. How long did they have before the towering structure exploded, sending missiles of death and destruction into the unsuspecting crowds?

Yvette and Jayce had insisted they not teleport into the resort itself. Jayce wanted Ellie out of harm's way—no surprise there—and Yvette was the main contact point for all news, so needed to be easily located. So instead of joining the witches in the search, they sat on a blanket in a grassy area calculated to be outside the danger zone.

"Ellie, are you sure this shield thing will work? We're sending an awful lot of people into a possible death trap with nothing else to protect them." Ellie strained to hear her. Yvette spoke softly, trying to keep her voice low enough to be undetected and loud enough to be heard over the festivities.

"Of course I'm not sure it will work. It managed to deflect a spell cast at us in the Witch Council chambers. But I've no idea how effective it will be if someone is standing next to a bomb when it goes off. But what other choice do we have?"

Jayce's arm tightened around her waist. "Elle's right Yvette. Unless we can track Thomas down, and manage to cast a truth spell on him, there's really no other option. Everyone has their senses enhanced enough to detect any unusual sounds or smells. So they'll either find the bombs before they detonate or have enough time to teleport out. Preferably before their shields are put to the test."

Yvette sighed. "I know you're right Jayce, but I hate having the responsibility of so many people's safety in our hands. I don't think l could live with myself if anything goes wrong."

Jayce's eyes darkened, his anger rippling through their bond. "*We* are not responsible for any of this Yvette. *Thomas* is the one causing the problem, remember? And every single one of those witches knew the risks before they went in. I just hope they're subtle about the evacuation. The last thing we need is for Thomas to suspect something's going on."

Frustrated at not being allowed to help, Ellie stood to

get a better view of the groups of people emerging from the entrance to the building. So far everyone leaving appeared to be laughing and carefree, and totally unaware the idea to go outside hadn't been their own. She grinned at the thought of their reactions if they learned they'd been spelled to think that way. Ellie just prayed they wouldn't run out of time.

A shiver of fear ran up her spine as the word 'time' resonated inside her brain. She doubled-over in pain, gasping for breath as a familiar sensation swept through her body. *Stars, not this again.* She dropped back to the ground, trying to fight against the nausea threatening to overtake her.

"Elle... what's wrong?" Jayce scooped her up and pulled her into his lap. He cradled her in his arms, pushing the hair back from her heated face, his brows drawn together in worry. She groaned, her stomach churning and her head pounding.

"A really... bad... feeling. Like... with Isabel." She ground out the words through gritted teeth.

Yvette paled. "*Damn.* There's something wrong with the plan. Remember last time this happened, we weren't meant to leave Isabel behind when we went to the Tree of Life?"

Ellie nodded, pain shooting through her head from the movement. "Time... something to do... with time."

Yvette gasped. "But we can't change time honey. What are we supposed to do? Is it something to do with a particular time, maybe a premonition that our time's nearly up? *Damnit*, we can't just... Oh dear Stars Ellie, you're a genius! We need to cast a spell over The Majestic to slow down time. Like we did with the Tree of Life!"

The nausea began to subside, and Ellie sighed with relief. She lifted her head and gave Yvette a grateful smile. Working out the solution to these damn feelings was like a game of charades! She shuddered as the last remnants of the pain and sickness left her body.

"Stars I hate that feeling! Lucky you're a champion at charades mum." She smiled as Jayce's breath came out in a loud *whoosh*. "Apparently, that idea will help. As long as Thomas doesn't realise what's going on of course."

Thomas

THOMAS SAT in a trendy little coffee shop, well clear of the blast radius, and checked the time. Only a little under an hour to go and the fun would begin. He loved the dramatic flair attached to the idea of the bombs going off at midnight on New Years' Eve. He never understood the mortal world's fixation with the date, but it served its purpose for him tonight. And the three-second delay between the explosions on each floor of the building was pure genius. Then, when they thought it was all over...

He smiled as an image of the beaten and bloodied forms of Jayce and the morwitch's mother chained up in his dungeon came to mind. Once he confirmed the morwitch and her friends were dead, Boris could finish them off. Initially, he planned to deal with Jayce personally, relishing the triumphant moment when the boy took his last breath. But the excitement waned at the sight of him already beaten, broken and helpless. Why sully his own hands when the previously defiant whelp had no fight left in him?

Catching the eye of a passing waitress, he ordered another coffee, adding a slice of the delicious looking chocolate mudcake he'd spotted earlier. He sighed, gazing across the moonlit water towards the supposed 'safe-haven' of his enemies.

Iridia would be in there too. Good! How dare she leave him and take refuge with this scum? But to be honest, he was relieved to be done with the insipid creature's presence in his life, and she'd saved him the effort of disposing of her without raising suspicion. But she would pay for defying him, nonetheless. All things considered, it was turning out to be a perfect day.

Jayce

JAYCE KEPT a close eye on Ellie, worried about these premonitions that seemed to strike with no warning. Plus, his own personal premonitions had kicked into overdrive. His dragon screamed at him to get her out of there. He wanted her somewhere safe, away from all this madness. But he knew better than to believe that would ever happen. Ellie would never agree to put her own safety above the people helping them.

Ellie had showed them all how to erect a personal shield, and he itched to cast the spell and join the hunt. Standing outside doing nothing, while the witches did a sweep of the building, was driving him nuts. He needed to be involved. They didn't even know how much time they had left. *Everyone* should be searching.

Jayce... you promised.

I'm sorry babe, but I can't stand the thought of you being inside if the bombs go off. Ellie had been reading his thoughts again. He should have known it was impossible to keep her out of his head. *Besides, I'm not letting you go in without me, and you won't let me anywhere near the place. So, it seems we're at an impasse?*

He nodded and checked the time. 11.05pm. So why was the crowd *growing* rather than starting to dwindle?

Oh. My. Stars. Dread washed over him as he quickly calculated the date. *This wasn't just any Saturday night. It was bloody New Years' Eve!* Thomas had chosen the busiest night of the year to ensure maximum impact. *Bastard!* And the fireworks at midnight would cause even more confusion.

Ellie clutched his arms as she read the thoughts racing

through his mind. The blood drained from her face as she considered the implications. No wonder more people were arriving every minute.

Elle, Thomas will have set the bombs to detonate at midnight. I know we promised, but what if we both go in? We could make sure we're out by 11.50pm at the latest. We might be able to make a difference, babe? We'd be shielded, and together at least?

Ellie chewed on her lip, her eyes filled with indecision. She'd been fighting the urge to help just as much as him. He gave her what he hoped was a pleading look. Finally, she sighed and gave in.

Okay. I don't think Mum is going to be too impressed, but you're right. The more people in there searching, the better chance we have of finding the bombs. But we need to be out before midnight, and you have to promise you won't let go of my hand! Not even for a second!

He squeezed her hand and nodded. She turned to tell Yvette the new plan, while he scoured the outside of the building. They didn't even know how many bombs were in there. Thomas would never leave something this important to chance. He'd want to be sure to inflict maximum damage. Nothing would be left standing.

The witches had already checked all the lifts. So far only one bomb had been reported found, on the ground floor in one of the cleaner's rooms. He figured there'd be at least one on every floor, so that left another ten or more bombs to find in less than an hour. Even though the spell had been cast over the building to give them some more time, Thomas would know something was up the second the bombs didn't go off at the scheduled time.

Jayce had wanted to scour the area for Thomas as soon as they arrived, until Yvette convinced him it was a waste of time. Thomas would no doubt be glamoured and could be anywhere. And until he suspected his plans had been discovered, he would stay holed up somewhere safe waiting for the show to begin. Exactly what he'd do when he *did* find out was anyone's guess.

Ellie turned back to him and smiled, a tinge of fear in her beautiful eyes. *Okay, mum's not happy about it, but she's given up arguing. Any ideas where we should start?*

He stared at the massive building in front of them. *Come on Jayce think. Where would you put a bomb where no one was likely to look?* The fire exits were out, they would essentially absorb some of the blast and lessen the damage. Somewhere not easy to detect the smell. So maybe around food? A memory surfaced of the night he ordered dinner for them. The waiter had wheeled in the portable table and set it up on the balcony.

"Damnit Elle... what if they're in the portable food tables! They're mobile, and no one would think twice about seeing them sitting around everywhere. And the food would mask the smell. They could even be inside some of the rooms. Stars, we need to send word to the witches to go through every room." He checked the time again, raking his other hand through his hair. 11.15pm. They were running out of time.

Ellie turned to her mother and told her Jayce's plan. Yvette's eyes met his as Ellie spoke. They welled with tears, begging him to keep Ellie safe. He nodded and grabbed Ellie's hand.

Time to go sweetheart. He blinked and they stood outside the door to Amos' suite. It was on the top floor, so he figured they could start there and work their way down.

CHAPTER THIRTY-EIGHT

Ellie

I t didn't take Ellie long to work out they were wasting precious time staying together. The hotel had hundreds of rooms, and less than twenty people searching. The thought of letting go of Jayce's hand made her stomach churn and her heart ache, but she buried the selfish thoughts and met his eyes.

Jayce nodded, his smile sad. *You're right Elle. We need to do this. But we'll work one floor at a time. At least knowing you're not too far away won't make it quite as bad.*

Okay, I'll start at the other end and meet you in the middle. I love you she said, and teleported before she could change her mind.

Ellie flew from one room to the next, amazed at how quickly she could move. The smell hit her as soon as she entered the twelfth room. A food trolley sat on the balcony. She was about to step outside when a searing pain shot through her head. She crumpled to the ground and darkness enveloped her.

Jayce

Elle, where are you babe? I'm at the halfway mark. Silence.

Sweetheart, answer me. You're scaring me. Where are you? Still nothing.

Familiar panic raced through his body. *What the hell?* Something was seriously wrong. Damn, he didn't even know where to start looking.

Wait... he could teleport directly to her. But what if it was a trap? What if one of the witches supposedly searching the building was working with Thomas? It didn't matter, he had to take the risk. Besides, no-one but Helena even knew he had his own magic. The old witch had turned a sickly shade of green when Yvette told her, and they agreed it wasn't something the Council would be able to deal with in a hurry.

He allowed the anger and fear that Ellie might be in trouble to surge through him. At least if he was walking into a trap, he'd have a power thrust ready to go. Closing his eyes, he focused on his beautiful girl's face, and the floor slipped away beneath him.

He opened his eyes to the overpowering almondy/oily

smell they were told signified the presence of a bomb. He was in a bathroom, a portable food table shoved up against the wall behind him. A dark shadow lay slumped behind the shower screen.

Ellie... Dear Stars, no! His stomach churned as he moved toward the frosted glass cubicle. Pulling the door open, he gagged at the sight of blood pooling on the floor. *Please don't let her be dead.* He hunched down beside her, groaning with relief when he found the weak but fluttering pulse in her neck. Without another thought, he scooped her up into his arms and teleported back the Yvette.

"Yvette, I'm sorry, but I don't have time to explain what happened. Please... just heal her and tell her I'm sorry. I need to go back in and find whoever did this." He ground the words out through clenched teeth, placing Ellie gently on the blanket and fighting the urge to stay. But there might be other witches left in the same state. At least he knew one thing for sure. This wasn't the work of Thomas himself. He wouldn't have left Ellie behind.

Yvette looked up at him, her face deathly pale, tears streaming down her face. "Find them Jayce. Make them sorry they were ever born. The witches found three more bombs, right where you said they'd be. The bombs are being teleported to the witch's realm to be dealt with as they find them. Do you think it might be time to put in an anonymous call to the bomb squad?"

Jayce frowned and looked at his watch... 11.25pm. "Give me ten more minutes. If we pull out now, I'll never find out who did this to Ellie. And please don't alert the other witches about Ellie yet. I'd like to keep the element of surprise up my sleeve."

Yvette nodded and pulled the blanket around Ellie's body. They'd been lucky enough not to draw attention to their comings and goings so far. The last thing they needed was for some concerned citizen to call the police about a girl with a head injury.

Jayce got to his feet as Jasper, Isabel and Iridia came running up. They were told to stay on the other side of the harbour. Obviously, they'd been a lot closer.

Jasper grabbed his shoulder. "Hell Jayce, what—?"

Jayce shook his head and shrugged. "I'm sorry... I haven't got time Jasper. Keep them safe..." he said and tele-ported back to the bathroom where he'd found Ellie.

He lifted the long white tablecloth draped over the trolley and spotted the plastic explosive attached to the underside of the table.

Jayce? Where... are you? What happened? A surge of relief ran through his body at the sound of Ellie's voice in his head.

Hey gorgeous. It's so good to hear your voice. You don't know what happened?

All I remember is stepping out on the balcony and someone hit me. But how did they get past the shield?

I think it might be one of the Council witches. She obviously worked out how to reverse the shield spell and leave you vulnerable.

A pause. *Jayce, I don't want you in there without me. Please come out. I need you here.*

Jayce clenched his jaw. *Sweetheart, I would much rather*

be sitting there holding you in my arms. But this may be our only chance to find out who did this. What if she's hurt some of the other searchers and left them to die? I can't just walk away knowing I could've helped them.

He heard other voices in the background and then Ellie's thoughts started tumbling over themselves in her mind. *Jayce, Iridia and Jasper have an idea. The Majestic has ten floors, plus an underground parking and the reception floor. That makes twelve altogether. And we figure the bombs are set to go off at twelve midnight. Well, Iridia reckons Thomas' sick sense of humour would get a kick out of the rooms with the bombs having the number twelve in them somewhere. What room are you in now?*

Jayce raced to the door and read the number on the outside. *Room 1512. Damn Elle... I think they might be right. Ask Yvette for a report of where the bombs have been found, and then a list of the room numbers. Oh, and send someone to room 1512 to get this damn bomb outta here!*

Ellie's soft chuckle was like music in his ears. He ran his hands through his hair and checked the time again... 11.35pm. When he looked up, a young witch entered the room, smiling as she walked toward him.

"I believe you have a bomb for me?" she asked, as if she were picking up the dry-cleaning.

"In the bathroom," he said, smiling back at the witch he didn't recognise.

She turned and headed for the bathroom as Jayce continued to pace the floor. *Hurry up Yvette, I need the information now.*

Jayce, Helena is on her way to get the bomb. She'll bring the list with her.

A cold shiver ran up his spine as he spun to find the previously smiling witch standing behind him in the doorway, muttering and waving her hands.

Damnit, she was conjuring a spell. Why hadn't he thought to ask Yvette how the witch could've reversed the shield spell?

Rage bubbled to the surface at the thought of this witch leaving Ellie for dead. A hard, implacable grin grew on his face as he let the anger and rage build to boiling point. She had no idea who she was dealing with. He was about to release the power thrust on the unsuspecting witch when her face went slack, and someone touched his arm.

Helena's eyes met his, and he saw the understanding in them, but she shook her head sharply. "She's not worth it Jayce. And she's of more use to us alive than dead. I need to know who's behind this."

Jayce nodded and reined back in the power. His shoulders slumped, and exhaustion washed over him.

"Go back to Ellie. She needs you. Everything here is under control now, thanks to your mother and Jasper. We found two other witches this one left unconscious as she did Ellie. I don't think this was personal. I think Ellie just happened to be in the wrong place at the wrong time."

"Thanks Helena. So are we up to twelve yet?"

Helena tilted her head, a twinkle in her eye. "All except the one on the first floor. Who knew so many rooms on the one floor would contain the number twelve? But it won't be long now."

She patted his arm, her eyes full of pride. "You've done more than enough. Now go look after that amazing morwitch of yours. I fear tonight's excitement is far from over yet. In exactly fourteen minutes Thomas is going to find out someone interfered with his plans. He's here somewhere watching, so we need to be prepared for the worst."

Jayce took a deep breath and smiled at the powerful witch beside him. "Thank you for believing in us Helena. Please let me know when it's all over." He cast a glance at the slack face of the witch he'd wanted to kill, now slumped on the floor in the bathroom doorway. Helena had been right to stop him. The young witch would undoubtedly prove to be just another pawn in someone else's bid for power. He shook his head and headed back to where Ellie waited for him.

CHAPTER THIRTY-NINE

Ellie

*E*llie jumped at the feel of the air shifting behind her. Then a pair of arms slid around her waist, pulling her back against a hard chest, and she smiled. *Thank the Stars... Jayce was here.*

"Hey beautiful. You look a helluva lot better than the last time I saw you. Sorry I wasn't here when you woke up." His warm breath tickled her ear, sending shivers through her body. She melted against him, covering his arms with her own.

"Stars Jayce, I was worried sick. When Yvette said you'd gone back in, I—"

"Sshh... I'm fine sweetheart. And I know I've said this before, but this time I'm deadly serious. I am *not* letting you out of my sight again for a very long time. How's your head?"

She raised her hand to touch the almost healed scar on

the back of her head, his lips nudging her fingers out of the way as he tenderly kissed the spot. "It's fine now. Yvette and Helena did an awesome job of healing me. So, tell me what happened?"

Jayce explained how he tried to message her, and when she didn't respond, had teleported to find her unconscious in the bathroom. She nearly choked when he told her about the witch arriving to pick up the bomb, *before* Ellie messaged him about Helena being on the way.

"Damnit Jayce, she could've—"

"But she didn't." Dragon fire flashed in his eyes for a second. "Although lucky for *her* Helena arrived when she did."

"But I don't understand. Why wouldn't she want the bombs found?"

Jayce shrugged. "Helena says you weren't the only one she attacked. So at least it wasn't personal. The Council will take her back to the witch realm and question her, but my guess is she won't know much about *why* she did it. Probably just following someone else's orders."

Ellie groaned. "In other words, just another stupid Thomas follower. How can they be so blind? Stars Jayce, what if destroying Thomas isn't enough? At this rate, we'll *never* be allowed to live a normal life." Jayce's chest heaved against her back. *Of course, he was just as sick of all this as her.* She tilted her head up and looked into his troubled eyes. "So what happens now?"

He lifted his hand to check the time and shrugged. "I guess we'll find out in about five minutes. When the bombs don't go off and Thomas knows he's been duped."

"What do you think he'll do?"

Jayce frowned. "When he came to see us in our cell earlier today, I saw the madness in his eyes. Elle, whatever heart or soul he once possessed is long gone. I've no idea what he's capable of anymore. Just pray that no one gets hurt in the temper tantrum he throws. Because something tells me there *will* be one." He leaned his head down on top of hers and sighed. "And you know I'll have to stop him if he tries to hurt people, right?"

Ellie nodded and pulled his arms tighter around her. "And you know I won't let you do it alone, right?" She tilted her head back again, watching the fear, anger, and worry flash through his eyes. He opened his mouth to say something, but the determination in her eyes made him pause, a smile lifting the corners of his mouth.

"Damn you woman, why are you always *so* stubborn?"

"Because you wouldn't love me any other way," she said, pulling his lips down to hers in a kiss that blocked out all other thoughts.

Thomas

THOMAS SMILED, the numbers on the electronic billboard counting backwards from sixty. His stomach muscles clenched in excitement, anticipation making his hands shake as beads of sweat rolled down the sides of his face. Swirling the amber liquid of his double scotch around in the glass, he sipped it slowly, as his moment of triumph drew closer.

Ten, nine, eight... the faces of the stupid mortals turned to the skies in anticipation of the New Year's fireworks. He chuckled... they'd get a lot more than they bargained for this year.

Five, four, three, two... Happy New Year. The word's flashed across the screen, blinking and rolling out over and over. The fireworks exploded into the sky, but he kept his eyes glued to the soon-to-be pile of rubble—The Majestic Hotel.

Thomas frowned, his stomach churning with rage as the building remained intact, its lights winking at him as if taunting him.

What the hell? Where were the explosions? Even if the first one had failed to detonate, the others should be ripping through the place by now. The whisky glass dropped from his hand, shattering on the floor as his hands curled into fists of rage.

No! This isn't possible! How... who? Blind fury shredded the last of his tenuous hold on sanity and he lurched to his feet, oblivious to the cries of outrage as his chair flew backwards across the crowded café.

Stepping out onto the esplanade, he looked around at the pitiful mortals gaping at the light display. With a loud roar, he morphed into his dragon form and leapt into the sky. He would kill them all.

Jayce

JAYCE STIFFENED as a familiar roar filtered through the noise of the fireworks. Dread settled into the pit of his stomach as a dragon appeared in the sky above the harbour.

Damnit... he wouldn't? Not here? As if in answer to his question, Thomas rained fire down on the heads of the unsuspecting onlookers, and Jayce knew what he had to do.

Not without me Jayce. Bringing Thomas down will take everything we've got together. *Don't. Even. Think. About. Leaving me behind.*

Ellie held firmly to his arm as he scrambled to his feet, looking up at him with fire burning in the depths of her beautiful eyes. He growled and nodded. *Fine. Let's go.* He pulled her toward a nearby carpark, looking for somewhere he could morph. Spotting a dark, deserted playground behind the parking area, he urged Ellie to move faster.

As soon as they reached their destination, he released his dragon and swung Ellie onto his back, lifting into the sky and heading toward where Thomas continued to terrify the fleeing crowds.

Jayce, slow down. I'm casting a shielding spell over us now.

Don't let him get too close. Ellie had sent the message using their own private telepathic channel. He nodded his large head and switched his brain into broadcast dragon speak.

Thomas... enough. You've gone too far this time. Why don't you pick on someone your own size for a change? Jayce hurled the message at the monster as they approached, and was pleased to see Thomas pause in shock at the last voice he'd expected to hear.

You! Thomas screamed, his voice snarling like a feral animal. *How the hell did you get here? I should have killed you when I had the chance. I won't make the same mistake again. Oooh and look, you brought your slutty little morwitch with you. Did you miss your daddy sweetie?*

Ellie stiffened. *Thomas, you're nothing but a sick mongrel who deserves to be put down. I thank the Stars your corrupted DNA doesn't flow through* anyone *else's veins.*

Jayce's mind filled with pride at his sweet morwitch's words. The message had served a dual purpose, reminding *him* that no blood bond existed between him and this insane animal. Thomas' huge jaws opened, and Jayce banked right as a stream of lethal fire poured forth from the monster's mouth.

Jayce, we need a plan. He won't be easy to bring down, but this needs to end here... tonight. He's crossed the line, and he's beyond saving. The only advantage we have is that he doesn't know about your magic. We need to work out a way to use that against him.

Well, I sure hope you've got some ideas, 'cos apart from breathing fire and trying to rip each other to shreds, dragons don't usually require any other battle plans.

Just give me a minute. I'm thinking here.

Jayce blinked as Thomas' image wavered in front of him then vanished, only to reappear next to them, roaring as he raked his talons through the muscles of Jayce's left wing. Jayce screamed in agony and tilted to the left, his useless wing falling against his body. Thomas was gone again before he could respond.

Thomas reappeared over the crowds again, unleashing another torrent of fire on the few people stupid enough to still be out in the open.

How's the wing you traitorous whelp? Did you really think you could take me on? My powers are way beyond anything you can even begin to imagine.

Jayce didn't respond to the taunts, struggling to keep them from spiralling into a rapid descent towards the watery grave below. He shuddered and breathed a sigh of relief as the muscles and nerves began to knit back together. Thank the Stars... Ellie had healed him.

His wing shot back out to the side, and he pulled out of their descent just in time. *Stars Elle, a bloody teleporting dragon. Talk about your worst nightmare. What the hell are we gonna do?*

Okay, I have no idea if this will work, but I can't think of anything else. What if you could combine one of the massive power thrusts you used on the wraiths in the underground cavern, with whatever you did in the cage to shoot fire at the wall. Maybe use your magic to hone the stream of fire into like a blade and then use the power thrust to push it out? Oh, I don't know. Do you even get what I'm saying?

Elle you're a genius. I think I might be able to do it. But I'm going to need your strength again. Are you up to it?

Of course I'm up to it. What do you think I am... a girl? But we'll need some sort of distraction. If he teleports in and attacks again, it'll drain too much of my energy healing you.

He had started to chuckle at her reference to being a 'girl'. Damn, as if he'd ever be game enough to accuse her of that! He froze as he became aware of other dragons around them.

You didn't really think we were gonna let you have all the fun did you son? Jasper chuckled. *I figure if we have to explain the presence of two dragons in the mortal world, we may as well go for broke.*

Looks like we got our distraction. But we need to move fast. I think even in his insane state, self-preservation will kick in when Thomas realises he has no hope of winning, and he'll be outta here.

Jasper, can you try to make him think you're scared of him. Ellie said, sending a message in dragon speak to Jasper. *Feed his ego. Make him think he can take you all. Can you do that? But be ready to fall back when Jayce confronts him.*

You mean play with him? I'm sure we can do that. Iridia, Isabel, you heard what our girl said... let's go.

Jayce stiffened when he heard his mother mentioned. *Mama? No, you need to stay back. He'll target you the minute he sees you.*

It's okay honey. I've been waiting a very long time for this, and I'm a lot stronger than he thinks. Don't you worry about me, you and Ellie just concentrate on finding a way to bring him down. His lapse in concentration when he sees me is exactly what I'm counting on. Just don't take too long.

The three dragons soared towards Thomas, who roared when he recognised Iridia's distinctly beautiful silver colouring.

Jayce. Don't lose focus. Ellie's soothing voice entered his mind. She was right. It was up to him to put an end to this. *Close your eyes and try to recreate what you were feeling when you did the two things, then merge them together. Picture yourself creating the weapon in your mind, then feed all the anger, pain and frustration into it. Are you seeing it?*

Jayce's head felt ready to explode, the pain like a knife twisting inside his brain. He nodded his head, unable to think through the agony.

I love you Jayce Raythawn... my energy is yours to use for as long as you need it. Ellie's energy exploded into him, obliterating the pain surging through his body. The weapon grew and began to take shape. It was almost ready.

Focusing his eyes on Thomas, Jayce roared his name. The other dragons dropped away, and Thomas turned toward him. His insane chuckle reverberated inside Jayce's head, fuelling the rage, and honing his weapon to perfection.

What, you ready to come fight your own battle now son, instead of sending these weak old people against me? Maniacal laughter filled Jayce's mind as Thomas hurtled toward them.

Jayce waited until Thomas was almost close enough to

fry them, then opened his massive dragon jaws and the weapon erupted from his mouth. Shock flashed through Thomas' mind as the flaming sword flew directly toward his heart. His arrogance had left him no time to retreat or change course. The fiery weapon found its mark, Thomas roaring in fury as the fire consumed him from the inside out.

Yes father, it seems you underestimated your worthless *son after all.* The words erupted from Jayce's pain-filled mind as he watched Thomas writhing in his final death throes, before plummeting toward the inky darkness below him.

Jayce. Ellie's voice was a soft whisper in his mind. *Sorry, but I don't think I can hold on much longer. Can we please land now?*

Jayce shook himself out of his stupor, fear clutching at his heart as he looked down at the water. *Elle, please hold on... just for one more minute. I love you Elle, stay awake for me sweetheart, we're almost there.*

Panic surged through him when he got no response. His body felt like it was made of lead. His wings were getting weaker by the second. It had taken everything they both had to destroy Thomas.

Yvette, his mind screamed in panic. *Elle's worn out. I don't know how much longer she can hold on. She needs you here... now. Can you—?*

Jayce felt the extra weight at the base of his neck and sighed with relief. *It's okay Jayce, I'm here. She's safe. Thank the Stars it's all over. Let's go home, eh?*

Best news I've heard all day, Yvette. He smiled as his

dragon family and friends surrounded them. For the first time in a very long time, he flew toward what he knew would be a brighter future.

EPILOGUE

*E*llie turned and gasped at the stranger reflected in the mirror in front of her. It was ironic really, how often this particular mirror had shown her a stranger. She stood in the guest wing in Jayce's family castle, staring into the familiar mirror with its unfamiliar reflection. She chuckled... at least the hair and eye colour were right this time.

She studied her reflection carefully. Her hair fell in soft curls to her waist, pulled back from her face and secured at the sides by diamond encrusted combs, a gift from her future mother-in-law.

Her own mother had supplied the exquisite creamy lace dress, adorned with tiny seed pearls and diamantes, sparkling like a million Stars where the light touched, and hugging her curves before falling to the floor.

But the most startlingly unfamiliar feature of the reflection, was the wide-eyed girl glowing with the euphoria of being surrounded by love.

So much had happened in the three months since that horrific day in Darling Harbour it made her head spin. *Thomas is dead, he can't hurt us anymore.* She'd had to repeat those words over and over in her head for the first few weeks until she actually believed them.

Oh, and the other one. *Both the Witch and Dragon Councils revoked the law against witches having dragon familiars.* That one had taken even longer to sink in. In fact, she still struggled to believe she was *safely* inside Jayce's family home, wearing a fairy-tale wedding dress and preparing to be married in the presence of the entire assembly of members from each Council of the magical realms.

"Oh Ellie, you look so beautiful. I wish your f-father could have been here to s-see this," Yvette said, coming up behind her and placing a hand on her shoulder, her voice catching and tears shimmering in her proud eyes.

"At least you're here Mum. And I know dad would be happy that Jasper will be walking me down the aisle." She reached up and squeezed her mother's hand. "I still can't believe I'm lucky enough to have *one* parent at my wedding; it's more than I ever thought possible." She smiled at her mother and chuckled. "And no tears, right? You'll ruin your make-up."

Yvette gave her a watery smile, wiping the corners of her eyes as the door behind them opened and Isabel, Iridia and the aunts entered the room. After a couple of minutes of hugging, with many oooh's and aaah's, the women pulled themselves together and Ellie drew them close around her.

"I am so lucky to have such beautiful, strong women in

my life. But I do feel just the tiniest bit sorry for my poor husband-to-be. Star's help him when we have our first fight." The women laughed and hugged, the love shining from their eyes fierce and protective.

They turned as one at the soft knock on the door, followed by Jasper's head poking around the corner.

"Is it safe for a man in there? We need to get moving sweetheart, everyone's waiting." He moved into the room and froze. "Ooohh, Ellie girl, you take an old man's breath away. Poor Jayce will struggle to stay upright when he sees you coming."

The women erupted into a flurry of activity and last-minute adjustments, before declaring her ready and rushing out the door ahead of her to join the guests.

Jasper held his arm out for her to clasp, pride and love beaming from his old dragon eyes. "Seriously girl, you outshine even the Stars today. I consider it a great honour and a privilege to give you away to a man I believe deserves you. And that's saying something." He gave a wheezy chuckle as they headed out the door.

Jayce

JAYCE FIDDLED with his bowtie and ran his hands through

his hair for the gazillionth time. Rhett nudged him, grinning from ear to ear at his friend's discomfort.

"What are you so nervous about? You can't seriously think Ellie won't show up," Rhett said, with no sign of the bitter angry dragon who'd come looking for him at Jasper and Isabel's house.

"Yeah, you got that right. I'm more worried I'll stuff up in front of all these dignitaries and Ellie will kill me. I'm so wishing we'd eloped about now," he groaned, and Rhett chuckled.

"Are you serious? Sheesh Jayce, you're rewriting the history books here man. The most important people in both realms are here to give their blessing on a union between a witch and a dragon, and you're wishing you'd slunk off like a mongrel dog and got married. If we weren't the centre of attention right now, I'd slap you sideways!"

"Hah! You'd have to catch me first... and we all know *that's* never gonna—"

All lucid thought vanished from his head at the sight of Ellie standing in the doorway on Jasper's arm. Vaguely aware of music starting to play, and chairs scraping as people rose from their seats, he couldn't tear his gaze away from the smiling vision walking toward him.

Dear Stars, his legs were shaking so bad he fought to stay upright. The sunlight reflecting off her dress was almost blinding, and he could have sworn a circle of Stars formed above her head.

Jasper winked at him, chuckling as he moved up beside him. "How're the legs going son?" the older man asked from the side of his mouth, and suddenly Jayce remembered to breathe.

And then Jasper placed her hand in his, and the dragon elder started to speak. But it was as if that were all happening to someone else. He remained oblivious to everything but the beautiful, feisty, sexy woman beside him, her face shining with her love for him.

He realised he must have inserted the correct responses and made the right movements when Rhett poked him.

"Damn it man, he said you can now kiss the bride. And hell, if you don't hurry up, I'll do it for you." Rhett's words snapped him out of his daze.

Kiss her? He was finally allowed to kiss his beautiful wife?

"Thanks, but I think I've got it from here bro." He pulled Ellie into his arms, soaking up the love pouring from her beautiful eyes. He kissed his bride, and the crowd erupted with cheers and clapping.

Ellie's voice in his head drowned out all other sounds. *Seriously? It took you like ten-seconds to even kiss me? We obviously need to have a very serious discussion later about my wants and needs Mr Raythawn.*

Jayce chuckled, grudgingly removing his lips and sweeping her into his arms. And then he spun around, roaring with laughter.

Ready when you are Mrs Raythawn. Bring. It. On. my beautiful morwitch.

End of Book II

FROM JENNIFER

Thank you so much for reading the Morwitch Series. I hope you enjoyed reading it as much as I did writing it. Originally, the series was only ever going to have 2 books, so the end of the second book left Ellie and Jayce in their perfect Happily Ever After.

However, I finally caved under the pressure and there are at least two more books in the pipeline. Without giving too much away, let's just say that the next generation of Raythawns should be interesting.

You can visit my website for further updates and release dates at:

jenniferredmile.com

I WOULD BE FOREVER GRATEFUL IF YOU WOULD CONSIDER LEAVING A REVIEW ON AMAZON .

ALSO BY JENNIFER REDMILE

The Children of When Book 1: Florisia

Kiss Me Katie

What Ghost

Nothing – Saving Magic Book 1

The Morwitch Series

FAMILIAR

MADNESS

CURSED